THE REDHEAD

Thank you

H M Howington

H. M. HOWINGTON

authorHOUSE°

AuthorHouse™
1663 Liberty Drive
Bloomington, IN 47403
www.authorhouse.com
Phone: 1 (800) 839-8640

Published by AuthorHouse   10/12/2016

ISBN: 978-1-5246-4468-0 (sc)
ISBN: 978-1-5246-4469-7 (hc)
ISBN: 978-1-5246-4467-3 (e)

Library of Congress Control Number: 2016916944

Print information available on the last page.

I would like to give thanks to my wife of thirty-four years for standing by me through all the hours spent writing and rewriting this book.

CHAPTER 1

It was a warm, stuffy day in Los Angeles. I had just finished a PI job that paid me a couple hundred bucks. There I sat at my desk, staring out the window and reminiscing about days gone by. Up to this point, life had been pretty lousy. *Chances are it's not going to change anytime soon. But what the hell? It's a new day. Maybe something good will come my way ...*

Then she appeared.

A tall, lanky redhead who looked like she had come straight from the angel factory.

She looked to be about five foot eight and had beautiful bluish-green eyes. Her red hair draped down over her shoulders, just below her grapefruit-sized breasts. I couldn't help thinking that this girl could be dangerous in a lot of ways.

Deep inside, something told me not to trust her, but still I wanted to know what was on her mind. Just knowing a girl like this could get a guy into trouble sometimes. I was hoping it wouldn't be this time.

She slowly walked toward my desk. I could tell by her beautiful complexion she had to be in her early twenties. I could have been wrong about that too, but looking the way she did, who cared? I knew in my mind

I had to help her however I could. Those puppy-dog eyes were too sad and beautiful to turn down.

"Can I help you, ma'am?" I said.

"I hope so," she said. "A man has been following me for three or four days now."

"You don't know who he might be, I presume?"

"No. I haven't been able to get a good look at him," she said.

"Okay, have a seat and fill me in on your problem."

She sat down on one of my old flimsy kitchen chairs that I had brought in from my apartment.

"First thing I want to know is: will what I tell you be kept in the strictest confidence?" she said.

"You can count on that, madam."

"Okay, I work as a secretary for the Jack Wortts law office."

"You mean the high-priced lawyer in Los Angeles? The one that advertises on the radio all the time?" I said.

"Yes, the one and the same," she said.

"How did you get involved with him?"

"I have worked for him for more than three years now."

She looked at her watch as she sat there fidgeting with her car keys. "Hey, look. I have to get back to work now. I don't want anyone to know I came to see you, okay?"

"Sure," I said. "I won't tell a soul you were here."

"I get off at five. I'll stop by then. Will you be here?"

"Sure. I'm here until six every night anyway. Here. Take one of my cards," I said.

"Oh no. I don't want anyone to find out that I talked to you. It could be dangerous for both of us," she said.

With that statement, I began to really get curious. I stared as she picked herself up from the shaky old chair and walked to the door. I was still watching her sway when she turned and said, "I'll see you around five o'clock."

Stumbling for something to say, I got up and followed her to the door. "I'll see you then," I said.

I couldn't help staring as she walked down the hall—casing the area around her—and out the door.

I made my way over to a window at the rear of the building where I could watch her leave. She opened the door to a new 1949 Cadillac convertible. It was a beautiful red with a Continental Kit. A Continental Kit was just a fancy spare tire cover that was mounted on the rear of the automobile. They were put on expensive vehicles.

I watched as she drove away and then looked at my watch. It was 1:00 p.m. I decided since I had some time to kill I might as well go to the local library and see if I could find something about Mr. Wortts.

I couldn't figure it. Why did she come to me for help? There had to be a lot of private investigators that looked a lot more successful than I did. After all, I did wear cheap suits and drive an old Ford coupe with a dull white paint job.

Maybe it was my six-foot frame and the fact that I was very good-looking, in my opinion. I kept my black hair short. No mustache. The one time I had a mustache, I kept picking at hair over my lip. That just about drove me nuts. Could be she fell for my deep blue eyes. I always got comments from the female sex about how blue my eyes were. Oh well. Just dreaming again, I guess.

It was time to get back to reality and go get something accomplished for a change. After stepping out of my office, I locked the door. Not that there was anything there worth stealing. My office was on the fifth floor in an old, rundown building with a broken-down elevator. The thieves I knew wouldn't climb that many steps to steal anything I had. I was getting a little tired of climbing them myself.

It would have been nice to have wealthier clientele. *Maybe, just maybe, this job is it,* I thought. I could still smell the expensive perfume Ms. Gorgeous had on. The clothes she was wearing had to come from some of the most expensive shops in Hollywood.

She was wearing a light blue skirt that came down to her ankles, with a jacket to match. I can tell you that she filled out her suit very well.

Believe me: I know cheap, and I know expensive.

I made my way into the parking lot where my old machine sat waiting like a loyal servant. I just hoped she would start. I always carried a pair of jumper cables just in case the battery died.

I climbed in behind the wheel, shoved the key in the switch, and turned it. She cranked a few slow rounds and then fired up once more. I loved the V-8 engine. You could get gone real fast with the power she had.

It was just a few minutes' drive to the local library, a small building on the corner of Gardenia and Tenth Street. It was an old, two-story building that had a Spanish look like so many other buildings around here. It could easily have been over one hundred years old.

It used to be the courthouse, until they built the big one close to downtown.

If Mr. Wortts had been into anything, maybe there would be something about it. I might need to search through a lot of old newspapers, but what the heck? I didn't have anything else to do.

I turned into the library parking lot, found a spot to put the old Ford, parked, and went inside.

The librarian was a short, slightly overweight, middle-aged lady with graying hair and a big smile. She wore the slightly overweight people clothes. The kind that had a lot of room inside.

"Hello, ma'am," I said. "Where would I need to look to find information on someone living today?"

"Do you have a library card, Mr.—?"

"Charlie McQuillen, ma'am. And no, I don't. Do I need one?"

"Only if you'll be checking out anything to take home."

"I need only to search for some information about someone," I said.

"Oh, you could start with the old newspapers."

She directed me to the old papers, where my journey began.

I spent the next couple hours hoping to find something about this high-priced mouthpiece. But I found nothing that would implicate Mr. Wortts in anything illegal.

Oh well, I thought. I looked at my watch. It was going on four o'clock. I had just enough time to stop by my favorite watering hole for a sandwich and something to drink. Maybe I'd be able to get more from Ms.— I realized I didn't get her name.

Fifteen minutes later, I parked in front of Maggie's restaurant. I walked inside. What luck. My favorite corner booth was empty. *Maybe things are looking up for me,* I thought as I made my way around the dining tables.

"Maggie, bring me a ham on rye. Bring me a cold one too."

"Okay, but if you don't stop eating ham, you're going to turn into a pig," she said.

How ironic, I thought. I'd been on the police force as a detective in the homicide division in Los Angeles for over fifteen years before the big war came along. I was with the intelligence department in the United States Army during World War II. That training also helped me in my work as a private detective. They taught us how to gather information about people without their knowledge.

Maybe I could figure out why it took Maggie so long to make a sandwich.

Then again, maybe not.

While I was enjoying my ham on rye, I noticed a story on the front page of today's newspaper that someone had left on the table. It seemed Mr. Wortts Senior was running for public office. A state senator, no less.

This put a different light on the whole situation. I wasn't sure if I wanted to get involved in anything political. That could get real dangerous. Oh well. Wouldn't hurt to listen to what the cute redhead had to say. After all, I did need the money.

Sometimes I think I should go back on the force, or I should've stayed in the army, but I was dealing with burnout when the war came along. The war gave me time to reflect on what I wanted to do. After the war was over, I realized that the military wasn't my cup of tea either, and that led me to private investigation.

I looked up, and Maggie was standing over me with my ticket. I looked at the ticket. "A buck and a dime. That's reasonable. By the way, do you know anything about this guy?" I said, pointing to Mr. Jack Wortts Senior's picture in the paper.

"I know they're private people," Maggie said.

"How do you know that?"

"Well, I dated his son for a couple of months."

"You mean Jack Wortts?"

"Oh no, his younger brother Peter," Maggie said.

"Hey—look, Maggie, I have to meet a client in a few minutes, but I'll be back later, and you can fill me in on what you know about the Wortts family, okay?"

"Sure, but I don't know if I can help much. They don't believe in airing their dirty laundry in public."

On that note, I paid my ticket and left for my office.

When I turned into the parking lot, I noticed the red Caddy sitting in the lot. The redhead was sitting in the car waiting. Just at that moment, a big black Buick came storming into the lot. The driver came to a screeching halt beside the redhead's Caddy. Before she could react, two men wearing black suits jumped out of the Lincoln, grabbed Ms. Gorgeous, shoved her in their car, and sped off. This also shed a new light on the situation.

It became very obvious that maybe the lady did have a big problem. I was thinking that big car must have belonged to Mr. Wortts or someone that knew him. There was no way I could catch them, so I decided to find out where Mr. Wortts lived. If it was him, his big Lincoln could be in the driveway, unless he put it in a garage. If that was the case, I'd have to do some legwork. I hated snooping around people's homes. You could get shot doing that.

The first thing I decided was to search the phonebook to see if Mr. Wortts was listed. I figured since I wasn't going to meet the redhead in my office, I might as well go home. I cranked up the old Ford and drove off. It wasn't much of a home, but it kept me from getting wet most of the time. Sometimes the rain would drip from the ceiling, but it was okay for an over-the-garage apartment. The old lady that owned the place was having a hard time making ends meet after her husband died, so she decided to rent the garage apartment. I was the lucky guy that answered the advertisement in the local paper.

I pulled into my drive and noticed my landlord Mrs. Kates standing on her porch.

I got out of my car and walked over to where she was standing.

"May I borrow your phonebook?" I said.

"Sure. Do you need to call someone too?"

"Oh no. I just need to find someone's address," I said.

"Well, come in and have a seat while I get the phonebook."

We walked inside. I found a seat on the brown, fluffy living room chair sitting against the wall. The furniture was old but nice. Mrs. Kates had mentioned to me before that they purchased the furniture just a few years after she and Mr. Kates were married. I remembered her saying, "We raised five children in this house, and it was a big job keeping the house in order." I looked up, and Mrs. Kates was standing over me with a book in her hand.

"Here's the phone book, Mr. McQuillen," she said. "Will you be getting a phone put in your apartment?"

"As a matter of fact after living here almost a month now, I'm having one installed this week. I'll also have the rent money on time this month. I made a real decent fee on my last job."

"That's good, Mr. McQuillen. I know it's hard having to pay your ex-wife so much money."

She was right about that. My ex-wife had a good lawyer, and he took everything, including the cat. All I had left was my clothes and the old Ford. I had to have a way to get to work. That's what the judge said anyway.

He was real generous with my money. I couldn't convince the judge that I was broke.

Mrs. Kates handed me her phonebook, and I began to search for Mr. Wortts. I found he wasn't listed in the white pages, so I turned my search to the yellow pages. Only problem was it wouldn't have his home address, and that was what I needed. I shut the book and handed it to Mrs. Kates.

"No luck there. No address for Mr. Wortts in the phonebook," I said.

"Who did you say, Mr. McQuillen?" Mrs. Kates said.

"Jack Wortts," I replied.

"Oh yes, he's the son of Jack Wortts Senior. Jack Senior was in the army. He spent a lot of time with General Eisenhower during the war. I plan to vote for him in the next election. Don't you, Mr. McQuillen?

"I don't know; I would be happy to find out where his son lives."

"Well, I know that Jack Senior lives in the only big pink house on Sherman Oaks Drive in Los Angeles. I know this because when Mr. Kates was alive, he was called there to fix a leak. My Harry was a plumber, and he was very good at his job."

"Are you sure about the house being the only pink one on that street?"

"I heard Mr. Wortts Junior likes to give a lot parties. He wanted his guests to be able to find his place with little trouble, so he painted his house a color different from all the other houses on the street."

"Well that's very helpful, Mrs. Kates, I'm gonna head that way and see what I find."

I said good-bye to Mrs. Kates, started the old Ford, and off I went.

By the time I arrived on Sherman Oaks Drive, it was starting to get dark. There was just enough light left to see a pink house. About halfway down, she came into view, a big, majestic-looking place fit for a king. Somehow I didn't feel welcome there.

I decided it wasn't be a good idea to park in front of the place, so I drove past, turned around, and parked on the side of the street. With a quick look around, there was no big, black Lincoln in the drive, and the garage door was up, revealing one empty space. The other space was occupied with an old turn-of-the-century automobile that looked as if it had been restored. However, in the driveway sat a red Cadillac convertible that resembled the one that the redhead was driving.

This was getting more interesting now. I wanted to know how that car got in Mr. Wortts's driveway. I knew I could go ask, but I didn't want to reveal myself to anyone just in case there was foul play involved.

This was going to require some serious planning. And it was getting too crazy to forget about.

The license on the Cadillac read CW6317, a California plate. I decided I had better get moving before someone noticed me. I drove back to my office to see if there was a red Cadillac still in the parking lot.

When I arrived at the parking lot, the redhead's car was still sitting there. This really put a monkey wrench in things. I drove over to the Caddy and took down her license plate number. I noticed it was very similar to the license of the Caddy parked in Mr. Wortts's driveway—this one was CW6318, also California. It looked like Mr. Wortts may have purchased both automobiles. It also looked like I would have to pay a visit to the courthouse and see if my suspicions were right.

I wished I had a pillow in my car; it could be awhile before someone showed up to move the Cadillac. I settled down inside my old car to wait.

Even though it was Southern California, it sometimes got a little cold after the sun went down. I was thinking, *I should put an old coat in the car just for times like this.*

I looked at my watch; it was showing two fifteen when into the parking lot drove a nearly new Buick. They pulled up beside the Caddy and stopped. All I could tell was it appeared to be a man that got into the redhead's car and drove off. I started my old Ford and began to follow them. I couldn't get the plate number of the Buick. He drove ahead of the Caddy, and I didn't want to pass the Caddy for fear of being found out. As far as I knew, they didn't know who I was, and that suited me fine.

We finally came to a large building on the corner of Aloma and Grand. The two automobiles turned into an alley beside the building. I decided to pass on by. I could always drive around the block and then check the alley to see if they had gone. I wasn't sure how dangerous the two people would be if they found me nosing around.

I drove around the block then decided to park on the street and wait. It wasn't long before the Buick came speeding from the alley and headed back the way they came. I started the engine and pulled into the alley.

It led me to a parking lot in the rear of the building. Sure enough, there sat the red Cadillac looking beautiful in the glow of the night-light that was hanging from a pole overhead. I thought I might as well check the front door of the building to see if there were any names on it. I figured it was probably Jack Wortts's office, but it did look a little run down for a lawyer's office. I drove out and parked on the street. A lot of traffic was driving by. I moved over and opened the right door of the Ford and got out on the sidewalk. To my surprise, the name on the door wasn't Jack Wortts but a name I recognized as a clothing maker. It was another piece of a puzzle that I wasn't sure I wanted to put together. Maybe I was wrong about the redhead. Maybe she wasn't dangerous at all. Maybe she just looked that way. Oh well, I decided. Time would tell—if she wasn't dead by now.

I decided I might as well go home and get some sleep and reevaluate my position. After all, I still didn't have a client to work for at this point. So no one is obligated to pay me for my services until I do get a client and a contract.

By the time I arrived back at my dingy little apartment, it was 4:30 a.m. I pulled to a stop in my driveway, removed myself from the old Ford, and dragged my butt up the stairs. I'd get a few hours of sleep then go from there. I got to tell you, those eighteen-hour days were getting pretty rough on me at age forty-two. I unlocked my door and went straight to my bedroom. I set my alarm clock to ring at eight o'clock. I fell onto the old army cot I had bought at the army and navy store for three dollars. I was asleep in no time.

Eight o'clock came quickly. It seemed like I had slept only a few minutes when the alarm went off. I got out of bed, did my bathroom chores, then made my way to the kitchen and turned the burner on under a half-full pot of coffee. Old coffee has gotten to taste awfully bad in my later years, but I still love the stuff and find it hard to quit.

I sat at my table pondering the situation. I knew I couldn't just do nothing, so I decided to look a little deeper and see if I could find out what happened to the redhead. I'd go back to the place they left the redhead's Cadillac and see what I could pick up.

I finished my bad coffee and headed down the stairs to the old Ford. She started up once more, and I was off. I figured I would stop at Maggie's and see what see she knew about the Wortts family. The morning crowd would be gone by the time I got there. I should be able to talk without too much interference.

When I arrived at the café, there was no place out front to park, so I drove around back and parked. I never liked parking in the rear; you never knew what kind of a lowlife might trash your vehicle while you were gone.

I knew Maggie always left the back door to the cafe open during business hours, so I opened the door and walked in. I found a booth and sat down. Maggie noticed me right away.

"Hey, big guy, what're you going to have to eat this morning?"

"Just a couple of eggs over easy with a slice of ham and a cup of fresh coffee," I said.

"There you go again ordering ham. You know what I say, don't you?"

"Yes I do. I always have ham with my eggs. It's a habit, and I don't see any reason to break it. Do you have some time to talk?"

13

"Sure. Just let me turn this order in, and I'll be right back."

Maggie was a slim lady with light brown hair down to her shoulders. She stood five feet four, 110 pounds, and was thirty-five years old. Maggie and I had been friends for about a year.

I don't mean to brag, but I still had my old army physique. I stood five foot ten and weighed 180 pounds. I got my black hair and brown eyes from my mother's side of the family. My adventurous side came from my father. He's been known to hop a freight train on a whim. I was told that one time he wrestled a bear when he was sixteen and won five bucks for throwing him. I think I'll leave the bear wrestling to dear old Dad.

When Maggie and I met, both of us had just gotten out of bad marriages. Maggie was married to a drunken bum that liked to use her to release his tension. Old Barry finally shot himself to death about a month after the divorce. I guess he couldn't stand life without her to beat on. My opinion is it couldn't have happened to a better guy.

Maggie went to the kitchen and turned in my order, then walked back to where I was sitting. I stood up and pulled out a chair for her to sit down. I was taught that a man should show women respect, and I hold to that idea.

"So, Charlie, what's on your mind?"

"What can you tell me about Mr. Wortts and family?"

"Well, I dated his son Peter for a short while. They're a strange bunch."

"Do you know anything about their business?"

"I do know that the old man Wortts and both sons are lawyers. I also know that the elder Mr. Wortts was in the army during the war. He served with General Eisenhower, but it's a mystery just what his job was."

"I don't think that has anything to do with the present situation. Do you know who the redhead is that works for Jack Wortts?"

Oh, that must be Leslie Carworth. Why?"

"She came to see me today."

"Oh? What did she want?"

"I never found out. She stopped by on her lunch hour today and said someone was following her and she wanted me to find out who it was.

"She was supposed to stop in after work and fill me in, but she never made it. Two men pulled up while she was getting out of her car and grabbed her. I haven't seen her since."

"Well I'll tell you, Charlie. I think you're better off not getting involved with these people."

"I think you might be right. The only problem is she may be in danger. I don't like the idea of bailing out on someone when they're in trouble."

"Listen, Charlie, I don't know if there's anything to this, but I heard that the red Caddy she drives was given to her by old man Wortts."

"Really? That's … strange. I wonder what the connection is. Why isn't she working for the old man if he's the one giving her gifts like that?"

"I don't know. Peter told me she couldn't even type when she went to work for Jack. Now that's strange—a secretary that doesn't type."

"Yeah, well, there has to be more there than some poor girl needing a job. I think if I find out what that is, maybe then I'll know why those two guys grabbed her in the parking lot."

"So, Charlie, who do you think is involved in this kidnapping?"

"Well, I'm not sure it was a kidnapping yet. I have no clue at this time, but I feel obligated to find out."

15

CHAPTER 2

I woke up Saturday morning with a slight hangover. I figured I must have had a pretty good time the night before because I found myself in Maggie's bedroom all alone. She had left me a note on the dresser saying, "Come on down to the café, and I'll fix you some ham and eggs. Thanks for a great time. Love, Maggie."

Slowly, the events of Friday night started to come back. We had gone to our favorite place for drinks and dancing. It must have been all the dancing we did, being I'm not much of a drinker.

I stumbled out of bed and headed for the bathroom. There was no way I could start my day without a good hot shower. I knew I had to find out what happened to Ms. Leslie Carworth. My inclination was she was in a lot of trouble, and I had to help her out.

After finishing my bathroom chores, I called Jack Wortts's office to see if Ms. Carworth was at work.

I was told she was out for the day. That worried me for sure. The phone company had no number listed for Ms. Carworth. I had no idea where she lived, so that meant I'd being doing a lot of gumshoe work.

Just then, my brain engaged. I drove to the café and had breakfast. Maggie gave me the redhead's home address. Maggie was acquainted with the family from a relationship with a male family member some time back. I promised Maggie I wouldn't do anything stupid. I always made her the same promise whenever I started a new case.

I drove to the address Maggie gave me. After a few knocks on the door, it was evident there was no sign of life anywhere. It was easy to open her door. I went inside and began my usual snooping around.

The only thing I could think of at the moment was that she might have information that could cause someone some trouble, and they had decided to silence her permanently. I sure hoped not; it would be a terrible waste of a beautiful piece of work.

I wrapped up my work there and started to leave. Before I could get out of the house, I heard noises at the front door. I figured it would be a good time to hide under the bed, being there was no place else to go.

I slid under the bed and positioned myself so I could see who was coming to visit. Just then, the door opened, and there she was … Ms. Carworth in person. The two guys that had strong-armed her into their Buick were at her side.

Well, that answered one question; they hadn't killed her yet. The way they talked back and forth, it didn't look like she was in much danger. I just wished I could hear what they were saying. I eased from under the bed and hid behind the door. I could hear their voices, but it was still hard to make much sense out of what they were saying. The most I could get was Mr. Wortts Sr. was going to run for state senator, and there was something about his record they couldn't get removed.

I figured I had better get back under the bed and wait until they left. Luck was with me. Ms. Carworth opened a desk drawer, took out a folder, and the three of them left. Whatever the secret was, maybe she'd let me in on it when she came to see me again. It was hard to figure out the deal with the redhead. What was she really up to? I thought I'd just tag along with them and see where they were off to. They didn't seem to be in too big of a hurry. It shouldn't be too hard to catch up to them.   I slipped out of the house and made my way to my old Ford. She started, and off we went. I could still see the taillights of the big Buick.

I followed at a safe distance, hoping they wouldn't notice me. I could tell by the route they were taking that we were going to wind up at Mr. Wortts Senior's home. Now I was really confused. Either Ms. Carworth was lying about someone following her, or it had to be someone other than the two goons she was with now. No matter, I had to find out what was going on. I was in too deep to bail out now.

I was right. The big Buick turned into Mr. Wortts Sr.'s driveway. I decided to stop short so they wouldn't notice me. The three got out of the car and went inside the beautiful mansion—at least it looked like a mansion to me. The house had three stories and looked to be over one hundred feet long and almost as wide. Forty-foot pillars held the roof over the porch. I was pretty sure they had more bedrooms than my house had rooms. The east end of the home had a four-car garage, and each stall had an expensive vehicle in it. It was obvious that this man was either rich or had one hell of a debt hanging over his head. While observing the surrounding area, I noticed what looked like a dark green vehicle similar to an army staff car, sitting on the street. Inside was someone obviously observing the Wortts family home.

Could it be the person that had been following Ms. Carworth? This would take more investigating! I decided to stroll down the street to see if I could get a closer look at the parked vehicle. I walked up close to rear of the dark green vehicle. Sure enough, it was an army staff car from the nearby army post. The tag number was too covered with mud to get a number off of it. I figured it was too risky to walk up and ask if I could get the license plate number. So I decided to get lost. I didn't want the army to know that I was investigating the Wortts family, or at least the redhead that worked for them. Not right then anyway. I knew from experience that the US Army wouldn't like the idea of some civilian poking his nose into their business.

I walked back to my old Ford. I got in, started her up, made a U turn, and drove to my apartment.

CHAPTER 3

I figured I could use my clout on post at the officers' club. I had a couple old army buddies stationed there.

I got up early, had breakfast at Maggie's, then drove to the army post. There were always guards at the gate. It didn't hurt that they knew me pretty well. I spent a lot of time at the club. They always had a good band, and that's where I spent a lot of Friday and Saturday nights.

The officers' club was called the Fox Den. It was a nice place to go if you wanted to have a few drinks with some friends and not have to fight your way out when you were ready to leave.

My guess was right. I saw Jerry Williams sitting at the bar. Jerry was an old buddy that I got to know in the war. He was in the same unit I was in, and we were about the same age. He stayed in the service after the war. Jerry was a trim 180 pounds, five foot ten, with blue eyes and almost blond hair that was starting to show some gray.

I walked up behind him, slapped him on the back, and sat down beside him.

"You staying out of trouble, Jerry?" I said.

"Sure! How's my favorite gumshoe doing?"

"I'm doing great. I was wondering if I could pry a little information out of you."

"Well, I don't know. Tell me what you got on your mind, and we'll see."

"Do you have any idea why the army would be watching Mr. Jack Wortts Senior's home?"

"Do you mean the high-priced lawyer downtown?

"That's the one."

"Not offhand. Why?"

"I'll give you the short version of the story. I was working on a case for a client, and it led me to Mr. Wortts Senior's home. When I got there, I saw a US Army sedan sitting on the street watching the home."

"I haven't had anything come across my desk about it."

"My client claims someone has been following her. She says she has no idea who it could be, and I thought maybe you might know something."

"Like I said, Charlie, I don't know of anything going on there. Are you sure he's one of ours?"

"I think so. He was driving an olive Dodge with military markings on it."

"Did you get a plate number?"

"No, it was covered in mud," I said.

"That could present a problem. Without a number, it'll be hard to tell who it was. Let me snoop around and see what I come up with."

"That sounds great. Could you keep this between the two of us for now?"

"Sure. It's just like the old days, huh, Charlie? Remember when we were dropped behind enemy lines dressed in German uniforms in late October? Remember how cold it was?"

"Damn right I do. We were the only guys that could speak German well enough to fool the locals," I said.

"We did come up with some good information that helped with the Normandy invasion."

"That is true."

I gave Jerry my new phone number and asked him to give me a call at home if he came up with anything at all. I drove back to Los Angeles, found a payphone, and called Mr. Jack Wortts Junior's office number. A very pleasant-sounding female answered.

"Mr. Wortts's office. May I help you?"

"Yes, is this Ms. Carworth?"

"No, Leslie isn't here today, sir. May I help you?"

"No, madam, I'll call her at home tonight. By the way, would you give me her home phone number? I seem to have lost the card she gave me with her phone number on it.

"Okay, sir, I guess it's all right. Just ring Klondike 2324." I quickly wrote the number down and said my good-byes.

The next morning, I woke to my alarm clock screaming in my ear. I had to have something real loud or I would never get up when I needed to. I hated early mornings—that was why I could never stay in the army. They think everyone should be up by five, and I think it's better to sleep until nine or ten o'clock. It's a tough life unless you're rich.

I called Jerry Williams's office early, and he informed me that the guy that was watching Mr. Wortts's home was an old boyfriend of Leslie Carworth. She had stopped seeing him. Jerry said the guy probably just didn't want to give up. So that looked like another dead end and a lot of my time wasted on nothing.

It was about lunchtime, so I drove to Maggie's cafe. I pulled around back and parked. In the lot was an olive

Dodge sedan with a plate number 6317. I went in the back way to the restaurant and sat down at a booth in the back. It didn't take long for Maggie to spot me. She headed for my booth.

"What's my favorite PI snooping in these days?" Maggie said.

"Just the usual. Looking for a good meal," I said.

"You see that army captain there?" Maggie said.

"Yeah. Do you know him?"

"No, but he was asking if I knew who you are."

"Did he say why he wanted to know?" I said.

"He wouldn't say why. He just said he'd like to hire you."

"Ask him if he'd like to join me for lunch."

"Okay. What are you going to have to eat?

"Just give me your special today with a cup of your fresh coffee."

The special of the day was usually meatloaf. Maggie always made extra-good meatloaf. When she had any left over, she would bring it home, and we would make cold meatloaf sandwiches. Just a little mustard and some hot peppers, and you had some good eating. It would play hell with my stomach later, but what the hell—you only live once.

I watched as Maggie made her way from the kitchen with my plate. She stopped by the army captain and left him with my request. He picked up his plate and made his way to my booth. Maggie was setting my plate down when he walked up.

"Have a seat, Mr. …"

"James Mudd, Mr. McQuillen."

The captain parked himself on the booth bench.

"Well, Mr. Mudd, what kind of trouble can I help you out of?"

"I would like you to shadow someone for me."

"Do you have a name?"

"Yes, her name is Leslie Carworth."

"Leslie Carworth, huh? Have you been following Ms. Carworth lately?"

"Oh no, sir. I wouldn't do anything like that."

"Well, Mr. Mudd, I have to tell you that Ms. Carworth came to see me about the very same thing. She told me she was being followed, and she wanted me to find out who it is."

"Like I said, Mr. McQuillen, it's not me."

"Okay," I said. I let it go at that.

I explained to Mr. Mudd that as long as I was working for Ms. Carworth, I couldn't help him at this time. He excused himself and left the building.

I figured Mr. Mudd was lying to me, but I couldn't figure out why. Oh well, I thought, time would probably tell.

I looked at my watch. It was going on eleven o'clock. I had to meet my ex-wife, Shirley, at noon at the home I had to move out of. There was no way I would meet her at Maggie's. That was my private place, and I didn't need Shirley invading my space. It wasn't my idea that we split up, but since it happened, I didn't need any reminders around to ruin my day.

It was a short drive to Pomona where Shirley and I lived for five years. Then came the war, and everything changed. I came home to a loving family, and then one year later, we got divorced. I still don't know what happened. Maybe I did change. Maybe she just couldn't love me anymore. If I could put all these maybes into an answer machine, maybe I would know what to do to fix it.

I pulled into the driveway at 615 Lazy Drive. The place looked a little run down since there was no man around to fix things. It was a nice place with three bedrooms and two bathrooms that we painted light tan when we moved in over ten years ago.

Now the paint was faded, and it needed a roof. I always loved the big oak tree in the backyard. It was a nice place to sit in the shade and drink iced tea after work. Shirley's only job was to take care of the kids and the home. Now she had to work a part-time job to supplement what I gave for child support—which, by the way, didn't leave me much to live on either. I was used to surviving on nothing.

The war taught that to me. I grew up hard and poor. We lived in the country. Thinking back, I remember we lived in a pretty run-down house that was barely standing. In the winter, snow would blow through the cracks around the windows. Needless to say, we would have to brush the snow off the covers before we got out of bed. I guess back then we never thought much about being poor. We thought more about what we were going to eat the next day. All in all, we grew up with little scarring, and our brains never suffered because of it.

During the Great Depression, my mom would walk to the neighbors and beyond to find work. She would do housework and most any other kind of work just to get enough money for a loaf of bread.

My dad worked in the coal mines in Virginia. The only vehicle he had was his two feet and a horse that was used to plow and double as a buggy horse.

Those were tough days that will always linger in my mind. I could go on and on about how bad it was, but what's the point? It's time to get back to the problem at hand.

I labored my way out of the old Ford and headed in the direction of the front door. Shirley was already standing there with a "Where's my money?" look on her face.

"You look tired," Shirley said.

"Just a little maybe. I've been working on a new case for a couple days now, and it's kept me up a little late at nights."

"I don't know why you don't get your old job back at the police station. It's a lot steadier work, not to mention steady paydays too," she said.

"Well maybe it's because I happen to like what I'm doing. Have you ever thought about that?"

I enjoyed being a little nasty to her. After all, she threw me out.

"I just think you could do a little better than you're doing now. Do you want a cup of coffee?" she said.

"Yeah, why not." I figured the tenth cup of coffee that day wouldn't hurt me.

As usual, the house was spic and span, and the radio was playing in the background. Shirley opened the cupboard and got a cup and poured me a cup of pretty strong coffee. I couldn't help noticing Shirley was still looking good at the age of forty. She was a five-foot-seven-inch brunette with dark brown eyes. And the fact she had two babies didn't hurt her figure at all.

I sat down at the kitchen table. We always spent a lot of time at the kitchen table when we were together.

In some strange way, I still felt at home there.

"Is this a dangerous case you're on?" Shirley asked.

"Not so far, but it's getting a little strange."

"What does that mean?" she said.

"Well, it started out as a civilian case. Then all of a sudden the army came into the picture."

"The army? It's not someone we know, is it?" she said.

"I don't think so. I really can't say much about it at this point. Anyway, here's seventy-five bucks. I'll have some more for you in a couple weeks."

"Thank you, Charlie. I know you're trying hard. I can't fault you for that," she said.

"Oh, here's my new phone number, in case you need me for the kids."

I wrote my number down in her phonebook because I knew if I didn't put it there, she would lose it.

I looked up, and Shirley was listening closely to the broadcast coming over the radio.

"Listen, Charlie—it's saying a man was found dead in a military vehicle behind Maggie's restaurant."

As I begin to listen, it ran through my mind that the man must be Captain Mudd. I couldn't remember if his car was still there when I left or not, but it had to be him.

The newscaster was saying that the name of the man was being withheld, pending further investigation.

I said my good-byes to Shirley and hurried to the old Ford. I was thinking maybe I could make it back to the restaurant before they moved the body and I could get a look at the deceased. LA's coroner wasn't known to be too speedy anyway.

As I pulled into the alley by Maggie's restaurant, I could see a couple of city police cars parked. I drove in as close as I could get without getting in their way. I could see John Garbor, LA's top homicide detective, was also on the scene. I decided to stroll a little closer to see if the body belonged to who I thought it did.

John turned as I was walking up.

"Charlie … what are you doing here?"

"I heard the broadcast on the radio and was curious."

"Do you know this guy?" John said.

"I don't know—maybe. Let me take a look at him."

"Okay, go ahead," John said.

John walked with me to the vehicle. Sure enough, the body belonged to the army captain.

"Well ... what do you think?"

"Yeah, I met the guy this morning. He told me his name was James Mudd. He was stationed at the local army post."

"How did you come to get involved with him?"

"He wanted me to do a job for him. I told him I couldn't because of other obligations, and he left the restaurant. I left a few minutes later. I never noticed his car when I left, so I assumed he was gone.

"What was the job he wanted you to do?" John said.

"It was a girlfriend problem ... nothing too serious."

"Okay, you'll let me know if you think of something, won't you?"

"Sure, you know me ... always willing to help the local cops when I can ... as long as it doesn't cause me any trouble," I said under my breath.

I left the scene with a lot of questions and not many answers. Questions like, was he the guy following Ms. Carworth? If he was, why did he lie about it? Or did he lie about it? Was he parked on the street outside of Wortts Senior's home, and if it wasn't him, who was it? Maybe Jerry could tell me more about Captain Mudd.

I realized that I still hadn't talked to Leslie Carworth. I decided to launch an all-out hunt for Ms. Carworth.

I wasn't sure if she was involved with the recent demise of James Mudd, but I had a feeling she knew something. I intended to get it out of her.

I found a payphone and stuck a nickel in and dialed Ms. Carworth's work number. I was in luck. She answered the phone and asked if I would meet her at the Club Cabanna on Wilshire Boulevard at nine o'clock. I told her I would.

I drove to the Club Cabanna, paid a five-dollar cover charge, and was escorted to a table. I ordered the cheapest drink they had. It still cost me three bucks. The Cabanna was a very nice club. There were crystal chandeliers hanging from a twelve-foot ceiling and seating for over 250 people. The floor was covered with marble tile that must have cost ten grand. The bandstand could accommodate a good-size orchestra, and the acoustics were out of this world. The kitchen was larger than what most restaurants had.

There was a main bar at the front of the building and smaller bars in each corner. The Cabanna was host to most of the well-known big bands that came to Los Angeles. It was 9:00 p.m., and Ms. Carworth was on time. I rose out of respect and seated her in a chair.

"Thank you," she said.

"You're welcome," I said.

"I'm sorry, Mr. McQuillen, that I didn't get back with you, but I won't need your services anymore."

"So you know who it was following you?" I said.

"Yes, and I don't think he'll be following me anymore."

"Why is that?" I asked.

"He was found dead today."

"I suppose you haven't a clue as to who did it. Right?

"Ah ... no I don't. Why would I?" she said.

The way she hesitated, I couldn't help but think she knew more than she was saying.

"Well, I guess that concludes our business then," I said.

"Here's fifty bucks for your time. I think that should be enough, being you really didn't do that much."

"That should cover it," I said.

29

I decided against telling her that her boyfriend tried to hire me to follow her. I thought it would be best; that way she might tell me more about what was going on. There was more to this than a jealous boyfriend stalking her.

Ms. Carworth left the building without ordering a drink. I headed for my favorite nightspot. I found a payphone along the way and called Jerry. He said he would meet me at the officers' club about ten thirty.

I had been at the club for only a few minutes when Jerry came in. I was sitting at the bar having a bourbon and water. Jerry walked up and slapped me on the back. I knew who it was. I turned around, and we exchanged greetings.

"Let's grab a table," I said.

We made our way to a table at the back of the room.

"Did you know the captain that was killed?" I asked Jerry.

"Not really. He worked in my building in another section. I saw him around a lot but didn't have much contact with him."

"I believe he was the man that was following my client ... well, my ex-client now. She fired me tonight.

"Yeah, she said he was. He said he wasn't. I believe he was. I saw him last Tuesday night sitting in a military vehicle watching her," I said.

"Are you sure it was last Tuesday night?" Jerry said.

"I'm positive. Why?"

"If we're talking about the same guy, he was on temporary duty all last week. I think he was at one of the posts back east then."

"Are you sure, Jerry? We're talking about James Mudd, right?"

"That's the guy all right. I saw the orders on Gus's desk myself."

"Well damn, don't that make you want to set a bucket under a bull?" I said.

"What?"

"Oh nothing. It's just something my brother always said when he was confused about something … and this is getting confusing. He said it wasn't him following her, but I didn't believe him. I figured he was just too embarrassed to admit it."

I couldn't sleep much the rest of that night. I kept trying to analyze what was happening and, if I stayed on the case, who would pay me. I guess the biggest thing was I felt I owed it to James Mudd to find out what was going on.

The morning was going along pretty uneventfully when the phone rang. I didn't recognize the voice on the other end. He asked if I would meet him somewhere. He said he had some information about the James Mudd murder and I could have it for a Mickey Finn. I thought five bucks wasn't much if the information was any good. He gave me the address and said he would be there at 10:00 p.m. I really didn't like the place he wanted to meet but said I would meet him there anyway.

At the time, I thought the address sounded familiar, and I was right. When I turned into the alley, I realized it was the same factory where the two goons left Ms. Carworth's big Caddy. I pulled in behind the building and stopped. It wasn't long before this big Buick pulled in. It looked like the same Buick the two goons were driving that night.

Two men got out and approached my car. I got out to meet them.

"You Charlie McQuillen?"

"Yeah … you the guy with information about James Mudd?"

"I got some information for you, but it ain't about the Mudd murder.

"Oh, what's it about then?"

"Let's say there's some people that want you to drop the case altogether."

"And if I don't?" I said.

The man turned to the other goon. He had the same build as the other one, maybe a little uglier and not much in the smarts department.

Goons don't have to be smart. The main requirement is to be loyal and follow orders.

"Harry, show 'em what'll happen if he doesn't."

Before I knew it, Harry's big fists were pounding away at my face. My first reaction was to drop to the ground and plead for mercy. While I was pleading, Harry was standing over me with a big grin that said, "There, little man. Remember this so I don't have to do it again." About that time and with all the strength I could muster, I slammed my fist into his crotch. He immediately went down. I continued to give him some of his own medicine when his pal started a new game. It was called slam his thirty-eight up against my head.

That jolt was hard enough to stagger me. He pulled the hammer back and shoved the barrel into my face. At that moment, I decided to listen to him. I would let 'em think I was going to play ball, but they didn't know Charlie McQuillen. There was no way I was going to forget this. I had good reason now to believe that one or more of the Wortts were behind this, and they must have had some pretty dirty underwear they couldn't get clean.

I got the Ford started and headed for home. The first thing I was going to do was get my own heat out of the closet and keep it with me. After all, I was licensed to carry a firearm and had a nice little short-nosed thirty-eight that was easy to hide. I thought, *It's my turn to ask some questions. And I think I'm going to start with Mr. Wortts Junior. If he doesn't give me some straight answers, then I'll make my rounds with the whole family until I do.*

When I arrived at my apartment, Maggie was just leaving.

"Don't leave now. I need some company," I said.

"I wanted to see you too. You didn't stop by for supper, so I got worried about you," she said.

I unlocked the apartment door. We went inside, and Maggie sat down at the kitchen table.

"How about a cup of coffee?" I asked.

"Sure. I think you make the best coffee in the world."

I put together a pot of coffee then took a seat at the table with Maggie.

"A couple of thugs tried to work me over tonight," I said.

"Did it have anything to do with the case you're working on? I told you those people are strange folks."

"They're strange all right ... I think into something illegal would describe it better. They told me to stay out of it or I could wind up deceased.

"Do you know any other people that worked for old man Wortts?" I asked.

"I know he's rich and he has a lot of people around him when he's in the public eye ... but why?" Maggie asked.

"I think the two goons that threatened me work for him. That's what I'm guessing anyway."

The coffee was ready. I got up and poured us a cup each.

"Let's go to the living room," I said.

I had only three rooms—a bedroom, a living room, and a kitchen. Each room had a nice big window. I usually left them raised. If you didn't, the summer heat could be pure torture. Bedsides, my apartment was like my office—nothing worth stealing there either. We retired to the sofa that doubled as a bed and sat down.

"Well I hope you're going to drop this case, Charlie."

"Not yet, doll. I need …" I was looking into Maggie's eyes, and I realized, *This lady is very beautiful.* I guess the fact that I really wasn't over Shirley yet had me blinded. I wasn't sure how Maggie felt, but I did know she liked me a lot. This seemed to be a good time to find out. I pulled her close, and she melted in my arms. We wound up in wild, passionate kissing extravaganza. The way she clung to me made me think she hadn't had any loving in a long time. I had spent the night with her before, but it was always a "I'm afraid of her / she's afraid of me" kind of thing. It felt good to break the ice. At that moment, Shirley wasn't even a thought to be considered.

The encounter proceeded to the bedroom. It wasn't long until I was undressed and tearing at Maggie's clothes. I was making great progress until I got to her undies, and she came to an abrupt stop. It was like she hit me with a brick when she said, "We have to stop here. Sorry. I'm still not sure yet."

I thought, *Not sure yet? Hell, I'm a desperate man, and I need some real hot loving.* So anyway …

I told her she was right. We put our clothes on and went on with the night.

I took Maggie home about midnight. It was a nice clear night. A night that made you feel glad you were alive. Maggie wasn't the kind to be up late, but for me, it was routine. I saw Maggie to her door. I waited until she went inside, and then I headed for one of my favorite nightspots.

The officers' club would be closing, so I wound up at Blackie's Place. I liked hanging out at places that were trouble-free. Blackie was a big man, about six foot four, so he could handle whatever problem came along. He wore his hair long in braids. He said he was Apache Indian, and I believed him. You wouldn't catch me disputing a man of that size anyway. I told Blackie my mother was half-Cherokee, which was true, so he looked out for me when I was in his establishment.

I hadn't been long chewing the fat when I noticed my former client sitting by herself in a corner booth. I looked up at Blackie in surprise.

"What's wrong with you?" Blackie asked. "You look like you just seen a ghost!"

"I don't know about that, but that babe in the corner booth there—she's the doll I was working for. How long has she been coming in here?" I asked.

"She started coming in here a couple nights ago. Before that, she's never been in here as far as I know."

"She's never been in here before this?" I asked.

"Yeah, I said that, didn't I?" Blackie said.

"She must be waiting on someone. I wonder if she's looking for me."

"You could send her a note or you could go over and ask," Blackie said.

"I guess you're right. There's nothing like a little personal eye-to-eye contact when you're looking for answers."

I finished my drink and headed for Leslie's booth. She seemed a little surprised when I walked up to her table.

"Miss Carworth, would you happen to be looking for me?" I asked.

She looked up at me with one of those crap-eating grins. You know the kind I mean.

"Huh? No. I was in the neighborhood and needed a drink, so I came in here," Leslie insisted.

"Yeah right. This is a pretty rough neighborhood for a girl like you to be in. Are you sure you're not looking for someone?"

"I would know if I was, wouldn't I?" she said.

"I guess you're right. Sorry I bothered you, ma'am."

With that little interchange, I headed back to my seat at the bar.

"I see that went well," Blackie said.

"Went well all right. That woman either has a screw loose or she's into something she's not talking to me about."

"You could be right," Blackie said.

"You know, Blackie, I would like to just get away from this one, but the more I try to get out, the more I get in. You know what I mean?"

"I sure do. That's how I got married for the fourth time. I just couldn't get out of it."

"What happened to the other wives?"

"You know this stuff I'm selling?" Blackie said.

"What about it?" I asked.

"I used to drink it instead of selling it. It makes a big difference what you do with it," Blackie said. "What about you, Charlie? I've known you a couple years now. You don't drink more than one drink. Did you have a problem with the drink too?"

"No, I like to have one now and then, and that's it. I never could get used to drinking a lot, except in the army."

"Hey, that don't count," Blackie said.

I looked at the clock on Blackie's wall. It was ready to ring midnight.

"I'm going to head home, Blackie. Kinda keep an eye out and let me know if that babe ever meets anyone in here, okay?" I said.

"You got it, Charlie. See you later."

I walked outside. The air was a little chilly. I pulled on my light jacket and headed for the old Ford. *I sure hope she starts. I still need a battery. There's a lot of vehicles sitting around. I bet one of them has a nice battery in it. But I'm not the kind. I guess I'll stick to praying for the old car to start.* Luck was with me again. I pulled her into low and headed west toward Hollywood. I had a friend that lived there and ran with the upper class. Maybe he could fill me in on some of the Wortts activities. It was worth a try.

I glanced at my rearview mirror and noticed a vehicle following at a distance. I usually wasn't paranoid about someone following, but I felt uneasy about this one. I figured I'd make a couple turns and see what happened.

Sure enough, he turned in behind me. *Not to panic. I'll just make another turn and see what he does.* I made another turn, and there he was, still behind me. *I guess it's time for a more evasive move.* I pushed the throttle to the floorboard, and the engine began to hum louder as the old Ford picked up speed.

It didn't take long before the car was up beside me. I pushed harder on the throttle, but she didn't have any more speed for me. I guessed I should have gotten her tuned up, 'cause I sure could have used some speed about then.

While I was thinking about the tune-up I never did get on the Ford, I didn't notice that the driver of the other vehicle had other plans for me. What I thought was engine backfire was actually coming from what looked like a cannon. I knew then I was in big trouble. Before I could get out of the way, I felt a sharp pain in my left shoulder. I knew I had been hit. Then with a loud thud, he smashed his car into the side of my old car. I immediately began to fight the steering wheel. With no luck, I lost control and was forced over a bank and wound up in a ditch.

The pain was beginning to get unbearable. *Maybe I can get out of the car and make it to the top of the bank. It's a pretty good climb to the top of the bank. That looks like a Hudson speeding away* … I think I'm going to pass out …

I woke up in a hospital bed with John Garbor staring a hole in me. I could tell he was real curious as to how I wound up in that position. He always seemed very interested in what I was into. He had visited me there before.

I figured I might as well break the ice and get the interrogation started.

"Good morning, John. How did you know that I moved into the hospital?"

"I saw the report. The description of the vehicle and the description they gave of the person. I just knew it had to be you. It sounds like I'm singing you a song here. Suppose you do a little singing yourself and let me in on what's going on."

"Actually, I'm not too sure myself. All I remember is I was driving toward Hollywood. I had planned on going home but decided to go visit someone. I noticed someone putting a tail on me, so I did a couple maneuvers to try to lose him—or her. I had no luck. Before I could get out of the way, they were beside me and started shooting. I went over a bank, and the next thing I knew, I was climbing toward the top of the bank. That's when I passed out."

"Did you happen to get a look at who it was?"

"I couldn't tell who the driver was, but I do remember—or at least I think I saw a big, dark-colored Hudson four-door sedan speeding away."

"The obvious question now is, do you know anyone who drives a Hudson?"

"I can't think of anyone," I said.

"Do you have any idea what it could be about? I mean it's pretty serious when someone tries to kill you."

"No, I draw a blank there too."

"Okay. When you get out of this place, come and see me at headquarters."

"I sure will. Say hi to the misses for me," I said.

"You got it. See ya later, Charlie."

CHAPTER 4

I knew I couldn't stay long in the hospital. I had to get out and get busy trying to find out who was trying to bump me off. Somehow I'd gotten in someone's way. I was sure they had no idea what I knew, and that wasn't much at that point. I looked up and saw a cute little nurse coming into my room.

She was about five foot two with very nice light brown hair and bright blue eyes.

"Good morning, Mr. McQuillen. How are you feeling today?"

"Great. I'm feeling great. When can I get out of here?"

"That's for your doctor to say."

"When will that be?" I said.

"Oh, he'll be in today. He checks on his patients every day. Now let me take your blood pressure. I have to see if you're still alive."

"I'm alive and ready to jump fences."

"I wouldn't go as far to say that, but you look like you're doing really well."

"Say, your name is Myrtle?"

"Yes, sir."

"You don't look like a Myrtle ..."

"My mom thought I did, and she's the one that was in charge of name calling. So I'm stuck with it."

"It's a very nice name. Could you tell the doc I need to see him?"

I no sooner made my request than the doctor came into the room. He was a big man with coal-black hair. He looked like he could take care of himself if he had to.

"Hey, Doc, when do I get out of here?"

"That's what I'm going to find out now. You look like you're good. Are you having any pain?"

"Oh, no, I feel fine."

There was no way I was going to tell him how much pain I was in. I'm not a complainer anyway. I hate complainers. Like my poor ex-wife, Shirley—she could complain about a gift from God.

The doc gave me a good checking out and pronounced me okay to leave. I can tell you it didn't take me long to get dressed. I figured I had better go see what the top cop wanted. John Garbor was not only a top cop but a good friend too. I met him early in my gumshoe career. I was working a case for a pal about three years before when it turned ugly. His girlfriend was knocked off by a guy that had been stalking her. John was called in on the case.

I didn't know what happened to my old Ford. I hoped she wasn't messed up too much. She was all I had to drive. I thought maybe I better call Shirley and see if she could come get me. She usually gave me her car when I needed it. I just hated to have her purr over now that I had been shot again.

I made my way to check out, took care of the insurance papers, and found a payphone. I called Shirley, and she said she would come and get me.

It wasn't long until Shirley picked me up. She met me at the entrance of the hospital. Just like always, she started giving me the third degree.

"Charlie, what have you gotten into now?"

"Nothing, dear. I'm not into nothing. May I use your car a couple days until I get mine fixed?"

"Well yes, Charlie, if you need it."

"I do need it; that's why I asked you, Shirley."

"I know, but you could be a little politer, couldn't you?"

"I'm sorry, Shirley. I've had a very bad day, and I have to go to the police station."

"Well, you could say, 'Thank you Shirley,' but no—"

"Shirley, please."

"All right I'll shut up, but you could say you're sorry."

"Okay, I'm sorry. Just drop me off at my place.

"Now there's no need to be nasty."

"I'm not. I just need to get some rest."

Shirley dropped me off at my apartment. I decided it was best to rest the day and get a fresh start the next day.

CHAPTER 5

Needless to say, a day of rest I never got. The pain was almost more than I could bear at times. The medicine the doctor gave me was limited in what it could do. All through the war, I never got a scratch on me. There was a time when it was close though.

I lay around the apartment until I couldn't stand it anymore. Then I called Maggie, and she came over. I knew I could count on her.

I heard the sound of a vehicle pulling into the drive and knew it was Maggie. I pulled myself up from the cot I had as a bed and made my way to the door.

"Hi, stranger. I haven't seen hide nor hair of you in a few days," Maggie said.

"Sorry, darling. I've been sort of tied up the last few days on a case."

"What's wrong with your shoulder? Did you run into a bear?"

"More like a cannon," I said.

"Is this the Wortts case you're still working? 'Cause if it is, I think you should drop it."

"It is, and no, I can't drop it. I've gotten too deep into it now. Is there anything more you could tell me about that family? I tell you what, this whole thing is becoming very strange. Why don't you see if you

43

can think of something while I try to find out what happened to my old Ford."

I made a few calls and found out that my car was at a repair shop in West Hollywood. It was going to cost me $122 to get it out. That was more than the whole car was worth, but what could I say? That old car was part of me. It would be like leaving an old friend.

I had a few bucks, so I talked Maggie into taking me to pick the old Ford up. We drove over to West Hollywood to Mason's repair shop. I went inside while Maggie waited in her car.

It was a nice little shop. It was also very clean for an automobile garage. I walked up to the counter. There was a short guy sorting papers on a desk. He looked up.

"Can I help you?" he said.

"I hope so. I need to even up for the bill on the '39 Ford you repaired."

"Okay. I'll get it for you."

He dug in the desk and came out with a bill.

"That will be … oh, I see you have the money ready."

"Yes, sir. How much damage was there?" I asked.

"Well, you took off the right fender, and you also tore out the A-frame. The A-frame is the part of the frame that holds the wheel in place."

"Yes, sir, I'm aware of that."

"Well, it's all fixed now," he said.

I paid my bill and followed Maggie home. She helped me in the house and put me on her couch. It was a nice place to rest. Her couch was more comfortable than my bed.

Right then, I needed a good place to sleep for a while.

I dozed off for what seemed to be about two hours, and then the pain woke me and reminded me what had happened. The doctor had given me some pretty strong medicine. It had knocked me out for six hours. I looked out the window, and the sun had gone down. I heard a rattle at the door. It was Maggie; she had been to the store and bought a few groceries.

"Can I help?" I said.

"No thank you. You need to rest. Besides, I have only this one bag. I can't believe the cost of food anymore. Of course it's not like it was when the war was on. Back then, you were lucky if you could get food at any price."

"I know what you mean. The war was rough on everyone."

Maggie fixed up a good supper. After that, we settled down on the couch.

"How about dropping me off downtown when you go to work? I have to stop and see LA's finest. John Garbor wants to quiz me about the shooting."

"Do you think it was connected with the job you're doing?"

"I believe it is. I'm not sure though. I just have to assume so."

I spent the night at Maggie's. She pampered me all night, making sure I was comfortable. Then we went downtown, and I gave my spiel to John Garbor. There wasn't much more I could tell him than what I told him at the hospital.

I dropped Maggie off at the restaurant. I decided I would go to Mr. Wortts Jr.'s office and see if I could catch Ms. Carworth. Maybe she knew more than she was letting on. She had something to do with it, and I knew it.

I drove down town to Mr. Wortts's office. I walked into the reception room where the office girl was polishing her nails.

"Slow day," I said.

"Yeah, they're in a meeting, and they don't want to be disturbed," she said.

"What about Ms. Carworth?" I said.

"Oh, she's in her office. You can see her."

I walked into Ms. Carworth's office, and she looked like she had just seen a ghost.

"You're looking mighty pale, madam. Is there something wrong?"

"No. I wasn't expecting to see you again."

"Why is that?" I asked.

"Well, because our business was concluded a few days ago."

"That's true, but something came up."

"What might that be?" she asked. I could tell she was getting more nervous. "Someone took a shot at me the other night."

"Why would you think I would know anything about it?"

"I just thought maybe you know something you don't know you know."

"I don't know anything. Now leave me alone."

I started to leave. Then I turned to her and asked, "Do you know anyone that drives a big Hudson sedan?"

She looked startled.

"I don't know anyone that drives an automobile like that. Why do you think I would?"

"It's just a thought. You never know what someone knows unless you ask. Assuming they're telling you the truth."

"I'm telling you I don't. Now leave me alone, please."

She seemed to get real defensive when I mentioned the Hudson. I was sure she knew who owned one. I said good-bye to Ms. Gorgeous and just started driving. The old Ford drove pretty good after the repair. *Maybe I should run it in the ditch on the other side*, I thought.

I decided that I would go to the brass and talk to Jerry Williams. I had no real hunch that he knew anything about what was going on. I just felt an urge to see him.

Jerry was busy at his job, but he could always find time to talk to me. He looked up from his work to see me coming.

"How's it going, Charlie? What happened to you?"

"I had a little class in how to duck. Needless to say, I failed."

"Are you still working on the same case?"

"Yeah, I am. I can't seem to get away from it. Say, do you know anyone that drives a big Hudson sedan?" I asked.

"No, I sure don't.

Just then, Gus walked up while we were talking.

"Say, Gus, do you know anyone that has a big Hudson?" Jerry continued.

"Uh, no, I don't. Why?"

"Oh, I had a little run-in with someone that drives one. That's all," I said.

"I'll keep an eye out. If I see one, I'll let you know," Gus said.

"Hey, thanks. I appreciate that. We should all meet for drinks at Blackie's bar sometime."

"What about Friday?" Gus said.

"I'm free," Jerry said.

"Okay, that sounds good to me. Friday it is," I said. Friday was only a couple days away, so I decided to go to Maggie's and rest. I needed some pampering, and she was always willing to do it. Living with Shirley had been just the opposite. I was the one always doing the giving. You sure get tired of that after a few years. I hoped that maybe by Friday the pain in my shoulder would ease enough to tolerate it without taking a lot of pain medicine.

It was finally Friday. I entered Blackie's bar and saw Jerry sitting at a booth. I walked over and sat down beside him.

"How's it going?" Jerry said. "How's the shoulder feeling?"

"Feeling pretty good. I couldn't swing from a tree limb just yet, but the pain isn't quite so bad now. Is Gus still going to be here?"

"Far as I know, he is," Jerry said.

"Maybe he can tell me more about Mr. Mudd."

"Who?"

"The army officer that was killed a few days ago."

"Oh yeah. I wish I could help you, but I never knew the guy. Maybe Gus knew him."

At that moment, Gus appeared. He walked up to us.

"Let's get a booth," Gus said.

"Sounds good to me," I said.

We found a booth and sat down. We had a few drinks and talked about unrelated things of the day. When I asked Gus, he said all he knew about Mr. Mudd was what he told me before. I had no reason not to believe he was telling me the truth. I decided that was probably a dead end. I would have to look elsewhere for clues.

Clues come in strange forms sometime. You get something that looks like a clue that turns out not to be anything at all. Then there's the kind that will be there, but you don't see it until it hits you in the face. So far, I hadn't had any of those to hit me.

After a few drinks, we decided to head to our respective abodes. It wasn't until the next say that I found out that Jerry had been in a bad accident on his way home. I knew I had to go see him in the hospital to see how he was doing.

After taking care of a few things, I drove to the hospital. I found out from the receptionist that Jerry was in critical condition. He was being monitored twenty-four hours a day.

Seeing Jerry unconscious and hooked up to all those tubes, I knew I wasn't going to get much out of him. Jerry hadn't drank enough the night before to be drunk. I guessed it was possible that he fell asleep driving home.

I decided I would investigate the accident myself. I figured the first thing I would do was check out his vehicle. I'd keep my opinions to myself until I found out more. I didn't think he was mistaken for me. He drove a red Mercury coupe. In the dark, it was possible it could look black. I had a lot of things running through my brain right then. *I better wait and see what I find out.*

I drove to the police station and went inside and found John. He was sitting at his desk with a bewildered look on his face. He looked up at me.

"You're just the guy I'm looking for."

"Why is that?" I said.

"Aren't you friends with Jerry Williams?"

"Sure am. Why?"

"If the guy dies, then this will become a homicide."

"Are you telling me someone tried to kill Jerry?"

"That's exactly what I'm saying. Do you think this could be connected to that case you're working?"

"I don't know. Why do think there was foul play here?"

"That's easy. We found bullet holes in his car."

"That answers one question for me. I'm pretty sure someone thought they were whacking me. I bet it was the same guy. Was there any witness around?"

"No, it was too late and too dark."

"I don't think Jerry has any enemies, so they must have thought they were following me when we left the club last night."

"Who did you see last night?" John asked.

"Just Jerry and Gus. Gus works in the same building as Jerry does. Other than that, no one I can think of.

I started to leave when I remembered. I turned back to John.

"By the way, keep your eye out for a dark-colored Hudson."

"Why is that?"

"That was the kind of car I saw speeding away when I was off the road."

"Okay, will do.

I left the police station not knowing where to go next.

CHAPTER 6

After hitting so many dead ends, I decided I had to look in another direction. I figured the person that was trying to kill me would get the job done, and I was not ready to go yet. It could have been that Jerry knew something he was not aware of. If that was the case, he might still be in danger. I realized I had better go to the hospital and see if I could get them to keep an eye out. It would be a bad deal to go through the big war only to get killed because of some stupid information he had. I turned the old Ford and headed to the hospital.

I went to Jerry's room to see if he had woken yet. He was still in a coma, so no luck there. I asked the nurse at the desk if they could monitor all visitors Jerry had. I told them what I thought, and they said they would try.

I really didn't like the idea of leaving Jerry there with just the hospital staff to watch over him. I didn't know what else to do. I still had to consider that someone could be after Jerry too. I'd just have to get John to put a guard on Jerry's room until he was able to look out for himself.

Sometimes that could be a real chore too. It isn't always an easy job to get John to do what I wanted him to do. I had to work very hard on it sometimes.

Jerry was my best friend. It would be worth the extra work to keep him safe. Besides, Jerry was the only person I knew that would come any time I asked. Jerry and I joined the army together We had a lot of close calls in the war and survived them. I was hoping this would work out the same way. I'm not a person to show my emotions but, I am very concerned he might not make it out of this. I would hate to have to depend on Gus. I really didn't know him too well. Gus didn't seem like the kind of guy that liked to have close friends. I may not have any other choice at the present.

I drove to police headquarters. I parked and went inside. John was sitting at his desk. He looked up.

"What is it now, Charlie?" John asked.

"I thought I might convince you to put a guard on Jerry's room."

"Why might that be?"

"I'm sure you thought about it and came to the same conclusion that I did."

"And that is?"

"That the attempt on Jerry's life might have been meant to kill him."

"Well, yeah, I did think of that, and yes, I'm sending someone as we speak."

John picked up the telephone and dialed a number. A voice answered on the other end of the line.

"Did you send that man to the hospital to guard that room like I told you to?"

I could hear the voice on the other end talking.

"Okay, I want a twenty-four-hour guard on that room until further notice. You got it."

John hung up.

"So, you see, I'm on top of things," John said.

"I thought you would be. Did you find out anything more?" I said.

"Nothing."

"I'm going to find Ms. Carworth. There's something that stinks about this deal, and I think she's got some of the smell coming from her."

"You could be right. Be careful and keep me informed."

"I always do, don't I?" I said.

I left the station and headed for John Wortts Jr.'s office. Maybe Leslie was at work. I had to get some information out of her, even if it was the hard way. I had to do that on occasion with war prisoners. I never did like it, but sometimes it was the only way to find out something.

CHAPTER 7

The old Ford turned slowly but finally started. *Damn. I'm going to have to get a new battery. With Shirley draining me dry all the time, it's hard to keep an extra buck for myself.*

I drove the seven or eight miles to John Wortts's office. I noticed Leslie's Cadillac wasn't parked in the lot. I decided to go in anyway and see if they would tell me where she might be.

I parked and went inside. I had a short conversation with the secretary. She told me Leslie wasn't spending much time around the office lately. That told me she was probably involved. What it didn't tell me was if she was in it deep enough to kill someone or if she was being used like a pawn in a chess game. I needed to find some answers before someone got killed or the trail got too cold to follow.

I drove around thinking about the situation and found myself at my old home. Shirley was standing in the yard, watching as I pulled into the drive. I parked, got out, and walked to where Shirley was standing.

"How're the kids doing?" I asked.

"They're fine, Charlie. You know I take very good care of my children."

"I know you do, Shirley. I just needed to see them today."

"They're with the Winslows on a picnic today. They should be home soon."

"Okay. Do you mind if I wait for them?"

"I guess not. Besides, I need to tell you something."

"What's on your mind now?"

When Shirley made a statement like that, it usually cost me some money.

"How much so you need this time?" I asked.

"Oh, it's not about money. I wanted to tell you that I met someone."

"You mean a new friend."

"You could say he's a friend. We've been going out for a month now. He's a captain or something in the army."

"You mean you divorce me because you said the army messed up my head, and now you're going with a soldier? How did this happen?"

"We just met in the grocery store and started talking. He asked me out to dinner, and that's how it started."

"What's this guy's name?"

"I'm not going to tell you. I don't want you to find him and get in a fight."

"I'm past that now, Shirley. I just want to make sure he's good enough for you."

"I might tell you who he is later. I want to wait to see if it gets more serious before I say anything. You understand that, don't you, Charlie? Besides, you won't tell me who you're seeing."

"I told you I'm not seeing anyone on a regular basis."

"Who's this redhead you've been chasing?"

"How did you find out about her?" I asked.

"Charlie, you're not the only detective in the family."

I couldn't help but wonder how Shirley found out about the redhead but said nothing about Maggie. I also knew that Shirley wouldn't tell me a damn thing if she really didn't want me to know.

"Did you hear what happened to Jerry?" I asked.

"No. What happened?"

"Someone tried to knock him off."

Shirley got a strange look on her face, like the one she got when she was hiding something from me. I wondered if she was getting her information from her new boyfriend. If that was the case, he had to be someone that knew Jerry. I wished he would wake up. Maybe I could get some clues from him.

"Well, doll, I got to go. I have to find a way to make some dough."

"I was wondering when you were going to give some money."

"I should be getting some money soon," I lied.

"Okay, the kids should be here soon."

It wasn't long until the kids arrived. We spent a couple hour together. Then I left for my office. I hadn't been there in a while. Maybe someone had left a note on my door wanting to hire me. *Maybe I should investigate Shirley, or maybe I should get out of the investigating business altogether. I have no other skills other than the law enforcement and the military. I sure don't plan on signing back up again. One war was enough for me.*

I drove to my office and walked the five flights of stairs to where my office door was standing open. I hurried to see why it was ajar. I sure didn't have anything to steal in there.

I pushed the door open. There stood a big guy in a suit.

"Are you Charlie McQuillen?"

"Yeah. Who's asking and how did you get into my office?"

"Your landlord let me in. I told him I had to see you, and he said I could wait inside. My name is Huey Johnson, and I need your services. It a matter of life or death."

"Sounds very serious," I said.

"It is. Someone's trying to kill me. They've been following me around for a week now."

"What makes you think they want to kill you? Maybe they just want to know where you go. Have you cheated someone out of something, or are you messing with some other guy's wife?"

"No, none of that. I don't know why someone would want to kill me. That's what I want you to find out."

"Okay. It's going to cost you though."

He reached in his pocket and pulled out some bills.

"I'll give you five hundred to start and whatever you charge per day or whatever you do."

I couldn't turn that down, so I took the big lug's money and figured I would shadow him for a few days just to see what was going on.

"Okay, I'll do it. I charge fifty-five bucks a day plus expenses."

"Fine. Can you start today?"

"Sure. Just give me a little information about yourself, and I'll get started right away."

I took down as much information as he would give me. I found out this guy wasn't too full of information. He did tell me that he worked as a bodyguard for anyone that would pay him well for his services. He also said he was working for someone whose name he couldn't reveal to me. That sounded a little phony. I was a trusting guy, but some people made me wonder if they were being straight with me or not. Time would tell, I guessed.

I shoved the bills in my pocket and escorted the big guy out of my office. I walked over to the window to see if anyone followed the big guy when he left. He drove off in a fairly new Chrysler convertible. That automobile would be easy to spot anywhere. No one followed him from my office.

He gave me a job but made it very difficult to do it. He was always sending me on wild goose chasses that led to nothing useful and wasn't even close to what the problem was supposed to be. I was smart enough to know a setup when I saw one. I figured I would just play along to see where the ride took me.

I did know that wasn't the car that ran me off the road a few nights before. But maybe these people had access to a lot of different vehicles. He wouldn't tell me where he lived, so I'd have to do some extra legwork.

I picked up the telephone receiver and dialed John Garbor.

At least my telephone still worked. *I had better go to the telephone office today and pay my bill.*

The telephone rang on the other end. John had a very loud voice, so I held the receive away from my ear.

A gruff voice came through the earpiece.

"John Garbor. Homicide."

"John, this is Charlie."

"Yeah, I know who you are. What I don't know is, why are you bothering me?"

"You know me. I like to keep Like LA's finest on his toes."

"I have plenty of work that does that. Suppose you tell me what you want, Charlie."

"Okay. Have you ever heard of a guy by the name of Huey Johnson?"

"Huey Johnson. Yeah, he's one of these guys that sells his service to the highest bidder. You don't want to get this guy mad at you. They had him up on murder charges but couldn't make it stick. Needless to say, they had to let him go. He works as a muscle man. He only works for the rich."

"Well, he hired me to find out who's following him. He thinks someone's trying to kill him—so he said."

"It could be legitimate. He's got to have a lot of enemies by now. But like I said, Charlie, you had better be careful. You can bet this guy is probably watching you more than you're watching him."

"I'll be sure to watch out for him. I intended to do that anyway."

"I know you're a nuisance sometimes, Charlie, but I don't want to see you get knocked off. I would hate to have to go to your funeral."

"That makes two of us. Thanks, John. I'll keep you informed on what's going on. Somehow I think all this is tied to Ms. Carworth. I think I'll go pay her another visit. I'll talk to you later, John."

I sat there awhile thinking about this deal. How did I get involved in something that might have gotten Jerry killed and maybe myself too? There was more to this than what these people were telling me.

At least Shirley would be happy. I'd drive over and give her a hundred bucks. That would cover the lie I had to tell her earlier.

I decided to stop by Carl's gas station and have him put a new battery in the old Ford. I never knew when I might need to make a fast getaway.

Carl had batteries lined up according to price.

"Which one do you want? I got them from four dollars and ninety-five cents to ten bucks."

"Give me the cheapest one for now. No sense putting a top-of-the-line battery in an old car."

"Okay, whatever you say, Charlie."

Carl went to work on the old Ford. I walked outside the building to get some fresh air. Parked behind some cars down the street was my new friend in the Chrysler. I walked down the street and stopped beside Huey's car.

"I thought I was supposed to be watching you," I said.

Huey got out of the car and stood me.

"All right, I'll come clean with you. But you can't tell anyone what I'm going to tell you."

"I keep good secrets," I said.

"Someone is blackmailing Mr. Wortts Senior, and I want to know who it is. I can't have my employer threatened and not do anything about it. You know what I mean?"

"Yes I do, but how is having me followed going to tell you who it is?"

"I thought whoever it is following me must have something to do with the blackmail. I follow you, and he follows me, and maybe you can catch whoever it is."

"Oh, I get it. Sounds like a hell of a plan. Do you know what it is they're blackmailing the old man with?"

"No, he won't tell me anything about it. He thinks it's someone who wants to ruin his chance at the Senate race this fall."

"Makes sense. Does he have anything to worry about?"

"Hey, you know lawyers. They make plenty of enemies."

"I see what you mean. Okay, I'll keep an eye open and see what I find out."

I left Huey and walked to the garage. Carl had finished putting the battery in my car.

I paid him four ninety-five dollars, plus tax. The old Ford started like a new car.

I drove off down the street with Mr. Johnson close behind. It sure was easy money letting someone follow me all day. Still, I did like the idea of having Johnson on my tail. He could cover my back just in case I got another visit from the guy that was trying to knock me off. I still wasn't sure that it wasn't Mr. Johnson driving a different car. I'd just make sure all the places I went were well populated. Besides, I had a hunch that these two deals were related somehow.

I spent the next few hours driving around town. There was no evidence that anyone was following Mr. Johnson. I thought, *This is just another lie from a deceitful bunch of people.*

I wound up downtown, parked in front of Mr. Wortts Junior's office. *I might as well see if I can't get some information from Mr. Wortts or, if I'm lucky, talk to Ms. Carworth again.*

I pulled off the street and into the law office parking lot.

I went inside and up the stairs until I reached Mr. Wortts's office. I opened the door and walked in. His secretary looked up from her typing.

"Can I help you, Mr. McQuillen?"

"I see you remembered my name."

"That's what I do best is remembering names."

"I'll keep that in mind. Is Mr. Wortts in?"

"Sure, I'll see if he can see you. What should I tell him it's about?"

"Tell him it's about blackmail."

I noticed she didn't get a startled look on her face. That told me she knew nothing about any blackmail rumors that might have been floating around the office.

She walked into Mr. Wortts's office. After about a minute, she came out again.

"Mr. Wortts will see you now," she said.

I went into Mr. Wortts's office and sat down.

"I understand you might be being blackmailed, Mr. McQuillen."

"Not me, Mr. Wortts. I have reason to believe that your father might be. Do you have any idea who it could be?"

"I don't have a clue. My father doesn't tell me much about his private business. He wants to spare us from any undo worries."

"What about your mother? Doesn't she ever say anything about what's going on around the house?" I said.

"She respects my father's wishes."

"Yeah, I know what you mean. My parents are the same way."

"Do your folks live here, Mr. McQuillen?"

"They live back east. Actually in the Midwest. They moved from Virginia to Ohio just after I was born."

"I guess that makes you a southern gentleman then."

"I suppose you could say that. Although sometimes I'm not so gentlemanlike. This business won't let you be sometimes."

"I can understand that. I hear guys like you have to muscle information out of people on occasion. Well, I can tell you right now you won't have to do that to me. I would tell you if I knew anything. I might just snoop around myself to see what I can find. I'll let you know if I come up with anything. Can I ask how you got involved, Mr. McQuillen?"

"It's a long story. Maybe someday we can have lunch, and I'll tell you all I can."

"I'll be looking forward to it."

"I'll be in touch."

I walked out of Mr. Wortts's office. I shut the door between his office and where the secretary was still typing at her desk. I wanted to ask her something without her boss looking at her.

"Where's Mr. Carworth today, miss?"

"Karin—my name is Karin Smith, and she's not here today. She's been missing a lot of work lately. No big loss."

"Why is that?"

"No one really knows what her job is here. She can barely type, and she's not good at filing paperwork."

"Why does the boss keep her around then?"

"I understand it's because of the old man Wortts. I heard that old man brought her here from England with her mother after the war. He said Leslie's mother was a distant relative of his. No one dares question him. He can get very nasty when he wants to."

"I'll keep that in mind while I'm sorting out this puzzle. Hopefully this little bit of information will fill in another blank."

"Let me know if I can be of further assistance, Mr. ..."

"Just call me Charlie."

"Okay, Charlie. Maybe I'll see you out on the town some night."

"You never can tell. Some nights I stop off at Blackie's bar and drink ginger ale. I had to get off the hard stuff. My doctor told me it was killing me, and I believed him."

"You're smart to, Charlie."

"Maybe I'm just afraid of dying."

"Not a big, brave guy like you."

I could tell she was flirting with me a little. I figured I had better get out of there before I made a date with her. Miss Smith and Leslie could compete in the same beauty contest. I didn't want any complications between me and Maggie. I kind of liked Maggie a lot. Who knew? She might be the next Mrs. McQuillen.

I left the office, got in my old Ford, and drove off.

CHAPTER 8

I drove along thinking about the situation I was in. It's easy to get in a spot but sometimes very hard to get out. I knew that eventually I would have to talk to Mr. Wortts Senior. I really wasn't looking forward to that.

The position he was in, that being politics, he could possibly make life hard for me. I didn't need anything to complicate my life any more than it already was.

I was pretty sure that he was into something or hiding something that he wanted to keep out of the limelight. I felt it was my duty to expose him. The last thing we needed in California was another crooked politician or one that had some heavy baggage.

I wound up at Maggie's restaurant having a ham sandwich and a cup of coffee.

There wasn't much of a crowd, so Maggie was able to sit and talk awhile. She asked me if I was still on the same case. I told her that I was. She got quiet after I told her I had to visit Mr. Wortts Senior. Maybe she didn't like the idea of me quizzing him. I noticed she wasn't talking with me. She was just listening to me.

"Cat got your tongue?" I said.

"No, just listening. I think you should drop this case. It could get very dangerous for you."

"I know. You said that before."

"This time I have more reason to say that."

This time I was the one that was quiet. I had to ask.

"Has someone been hassling you?"

"You could say that. Please don't ask me who it was. They called me on the telephone and told me to keep my mouth shut, and if I didn't, they would make sure I never talked again. I asked him who he was, and he said I would find out if I ever said anything to anyone."

As much as I wanted to know, I had to think of Maggie's safety. Besides, I was pretty sure I knew who they were. I just didn't know which one of them made the threat.

I was going to keep looking until I found the redhead. I figured she had a lot of keys that fit a lot of locks that were hiding a lot of dirty little secrets involving the case. I just had to be more discreet in getting the information I needed.

I could tell she was scared, so I tried to reassure her that these people were just a bunch of blowhards, and they couldn't afford to do anything stupid.

"Maybe you're right, but I still don't like taking any chances," she said.

"I tell you what. I'll stay with you until this thing has passed. That way I can protect you."

"Okay, that would make me feel better."

"I'll sleep on your couch. If anyone tries to open your door, I'll be able to hear them."

"What about the windows?"

"I guess we could put bars over them. That neighborhood you live in isn't too safe these days anyway."

"I know. I've been wanting to move to a better area anyway. I was hoping that my restaurant would get well known, and I would have a full house every day."

"Give it time. You're a good cook. You have the best food in the entire area. What do you think made me keep coming back here? It was your beautiful smile and the great food you serve."

"Don't tell me that. All you order is ham and meatloaf sandwiches."

"And very good sandwiches they are. I tell you what. I'm still hungry. What is your special today?"

"You get two pork chops, mashed potatoes, and green beans for one dollar and a quarter."

"Okay, set me up."

Maggie brought me the special. I sat there and ate like a hungry hog. I didn't realize how starved I was.

I hung around until closing time. I drove to my place and had Maggie pick me up. I got my .45-caliber pistol and a change of clothes and drove Maggie's car back to her place. Maggie had a 1938 red, two-door Plymouth coupe. She said she loved red automobiles. Her husband had bought it for her just after they were married. I guess he did do one good thing for her.

I figured I would spend the daylight hours chasing suspects, and my nights I would spend with Maggie. That way, anyone messing around her house would get a big surprise. I didn't worry about the daylight hours inside the restaurant. They would be crazy to try something there. I had to keep in mind that someone knocked off Mr. Mudd behind Maggie's restaurant in broad daylight. I wasn't sure if the two were really connected. Whoever knocked him off may not have had anything to do with the Wortts. I learned one thing in this business, and that is to never rule anything out or vice versa. Things have a way of crossing you up. You just never know what will happen next.

CHAPTER 9

It was a quiet night at Maggie's. We got up and had a good shower. I drove Maggie to the restaurant. She made me a good breakfast of ham and eggs with a cup of her great-tasting coffee. I think I must have drunk a whole pot by myself. I sure wanted to top that off with a good cigarette, but I knew I had to stay off them. The combination of cigarettes and alcohol was killing me, so my doctor told me. I did find it strange that every time I went in to see the good doctor, he smelled like he just had a smoke himself. Of course, we all know it doesn't apply to doctors.

I looked up from my plate to see Maggie standing over me with the coffee pot in her hand.

"Like some more coffee, Charlie?"

"No, darling. I think I'm coffee'd up."

"What are your plans for today?"

"Don't worry your pretty little head. I promise I won't get in any trouble."

I didn't want to tell her I planned on finding Mr. Wortts Senior and squeezing some information out of him.

"I'll pick you up after closing tonight."

"Okay. Can you get here a little early? Say, before dark?"

"Sure. Maybe you should have Helen close for you. Just until I get this thing solved."

"I thought you told me you were going to stay out of it."

Oops, I didn't mean to say that.

"Well, I meant to say until John solves it. You know we can't keep on hiding forever."

"I know, Charlie. I'm just scared that something might happen to you. You know how I worry, don't you?"

"Yes, you have made that pretty clear. I promise I won't let anything happen to either one of us. You can count on that."

I finished breakfast and headed out to find Mr. Wortts Senior.

I decided to try his office first. He had a plush office downtown in the ritzy part of Los Angeles.

It seemed Mr. Wortts came from a long line of lawyers. I guess that's how they became so rich. He made a lot of dough counseling the rich Hollywood folks. *Maybe I should become their private gumshoe,* I thought. *Mr. Wortts could throw some work my way. That would be nice. I guess I had better not get ahead of myself. He could be involved in this thing clean up to his ears.*

First things are first, and the first thing there was to find out how deeply he was in the blackmail. I had Wortts Senior and Wortts Junior, who claimed he knew nothing about any blackmail. Mrs. Carworth and her two thugs, and the murder of an army officer.

I couldn't forget Maggie being threatened and Jerry lying in a coma in the hospital. That made for a strange pot of soup, and it was very hard to figure out all the ingredients. *I guess I'll have to keep separating the vegetables until I find what kind of meat there is in it.*

I arrived at the law office of Mr. Wortts Senior. It was a very impressive place. They had their own parking lot just for them and customers.

My old Ford looked out of place among all the expensive vehicles sitting there. I noticed a red Caddy convertible sitting there. Could I have lucked out and found Ms. Carworth too?

I took the elevator up to the fourth floor and found office 410. I opened the door and walked in. There was another beautiful secretary sitting at her desk. She was a strawberry blonde with very big hazel eyes. She looked to be about five foot two or three. She was wearing a tight lavender skirt with a pink pullover sweater and white high-heel shoes. *I guess Hollywood doesn't have all the beauties after all.*

The furniture looked like it cost more than my house. I would have bet the secretary's desk cost over a thousand bucks. There were two chairs that would go for three or four hundred dollars each.

She looked up from her work.

"Do you have an appointment, Mr. …"

"McQuillen, Charlie McQuillen, and no I don't. I was just hoping to talk to Mr. Wortts about a very important matter."

"I'm not sure if he can see you now. He's a very busy man, you know."

"Yes, I do, but I was hoping to talk to him about a blackmail."

The babe looked startled when I mentioned blackmail. Kind of like I might have hit a nerve.

"Blackmail? Are you saying you're being blackmailed, Mr. McQuillen?"

"Not me. I think your boss is being blackmailed."

"Oh, I see. I thought you meant that you were being blackmailed."

"Somehow I doubt that, darling. You're the second person that asked me that."

"I'll see if he can see you."

She got up and opened a big door to another office. She walked in and shut the door behind her. She must have stayed in his office for fifteen minutes. I was getting tired of waiting when the door opened and she came out.

"Mr. Wortts will see you now."

I thanked her and walked through the big door into Wortts's office.

I just about passed out at the sight of his office.

I noticed all his furniture was made of white maple. The reason I knew this was because I had a friend that worked with wood. He gave me the lowdown on a lot of different types of wood and how expensive they are. I can tell you that white maple is very expensive.

Mr. Wortts stood up from his desk. He was a thin man, about six foot two. He had thin gray hair cut very short. I guess it's the military discipline that a lot of guys stay with after they leave the service. I prefer longer hair. He was wearing a green double-breasted pinstripe suit. I would have bet that suit cost over three hundred bucks, and his shoes must have cost him at least fifty.

"Nice desk you have there," I said.

"I bought it and had it shipped to me from England. I paid ten thousand dollars for it."

It took me a minute before I could think of anything to say. I figured it was expensive, but that was way out there.

"It's very nice."

"I have to keep up a very high-profile look in order to let my type of customer know that I'm extremely successful, if you know what I mean. What is it you need from me, Mr. McQuillen?"

"Oh, just a little information mixed with a lot of truth."

"Do you assume all lawyers are liars, Mr. McQuillen?"

"No, I don't. It's the man that lies. I believe in letting a person establish what he is himself."

"My secretary tells me you want some information about a blackmail. Mine in particular. Yes, it is true I'm having a problem. There's nothing you can do to help me. Besides, I can handle it myself."

"Well, the reason I got involved is because your son's lovely secretary came to me and wanted me to find out who was following her. She said in a word that she thought someone was trying to kill her. Which turned out not to be the case. The guy I thought was following her turned up dead one day. I won't bore you with the details of how I got to this point, but this is where we're at right now."

"What all do you know about my son's secretary?"

"Not much. She has been avoiding me since Mr. Mudd turned up dead. I do know that you got your son to hire her. I know she was dating Mr. Mudd. You wouldn't happen to know anything about the Mudd's murder, would you?"

"I assure you, sir, I had nothing to do with it—nor do I know anything about it."

"I trust you are telling me the truth. Can I ask you another question?"

"I may have to charge you one hundred dollars an hour if you stay too much longer. Go ahead—ask."

"What is your connection with Ms. Carworth?"

"You're digging a little too deep in my business with that question. This is a very personal matter I don't intend go into."

"Do you employ a man by the name of Huey Johnson?"

"As a matter of fact, I do. Why?"

"He hired me to find out who's blackmailing you."

"Mr. McQuillen, you don't have to worry yourself about me being blackmailed. It's not a problem to me right now."

"So you're saying that this blackmail really isn't blackmail at all."

"Yes, you can put it that way. The person that is threatening me has realized they have no power over me and decided to give it up."

"Well, I guess that's good news for you, but it doesn't solve anything for me. I still have to find who's trying to kill me. I won't take up any more of your time, sir."

"Maybe you could do some investigating for me. I need a good investigator now and again."

"You never know. I'll give it a think when I clear up this case. Good say, sir."

I walked out of Mr. Wortts's office to where his secretary was at work. She looked and gave me a big grin. I smiled and kept on walking. No need to cause myself any more trouble than I had already.

Somehow I just couldn't believe Mr. Wortts was giving me the real story. I learned how to read people while working in intelligence for the army. Mr. Wortts wasn't reading to well.

Maybe the blackmailer was Mudd, and Wortts had him knocked off to keep him quiet. Anything was possible.

CHAPTER 10

I decided to drive a block or two from Mr. Wortts's home and wait to see if I could catch a glimpse of Ms. Carworth leaving.

I must have waited there for three hours, but it paid off.

I watched as she came out of the house and got into her Caddy and drove off. Those military binoculars did come in handy in my profession.

I stayed a few cars behind her just in case. If she saw me, she might lead me on a wild goose chase, and there was one thing I didn't need—another wild goose chase.

So far my luck was holding up. She hadn't spotted me so far. I followed her what must have been a good ten miles going nowhere. I realized she must have spotted me somehow. I picked up speed, passed a few cars, and cut her off. She pulled to a stop and jumped out of her car. I pulled in behind her and got out of my car.

"What are you trying to do—kill me?" she said.

"No, madam. I just want some answers from you. I prefer truthful ones."

"I told you I don't know anything."

"I believe you do, and I'm going to find out what it is if I have to beat it out of you."

"All right, you don't have to do that. What is it you want to know?"

"For starters, I would like to know what your relationship to Mr. Wortts Senior is."

"I'm his illegitimate daughter, okay?"

All of a sudden, things got a lot clearer to me.

"When did you come into the picture?" I asked.

"A couple of years ago. I was born in England during World War One. My mother was a civilian working for the American Army in London. That's where my father met my mother. They couldn't get married because my father had a wife and son in America. My mother got pregnant with me, and when she told him about it, he informed her he was already married. He promised to take good care of her, which he did. He sent her money each month until I reached eighteen years old. I never knew him. All I ever saw was a photograph that she kept of him. I found out he was a rich lawyer from California. I decided to go to America and find my dear old dad. You know, a girl should know her father. Don't you think so, Mr. McQuillen?"

"Yes, I believe a girl should know her father, but I don't think she should blackmail him. Isn't that what you're doing, Ms. Carworth?"

"I wouldn't call it that."

"That's funny. That's the same thing he said. Aren't you forcing him to pay you to keep quiet? I assume Mrs. Wortts doesn't know about you."

"That's where you're wrong. She knows, but their two sons and daughter don't. He told me he would take good care of me after the election. I just have to keep quiet about being his daughter. He said no one can ever find out."

"How does that make you feel, taking a backseat to his other children? Are you in his will?"

"Actually, no. He said if the press got hold of a story like that, he would never be elected."

"He's right about that. What about Mudd? How does he figure in this and why would someone want to knock him off?"

"I told you I don't know why. I went out with him a few times. That's all there was to that. He must have been the one that was following me because after he died, I was no longer followed. I figured he was the one that was stalking me."

"Would it interest you to know that Mr. Mudd was back east on assignment for the army at the time you told me you were being followed?"

When I told her that, her peachy colored skin turned pale white. I wasn't sure how to read that.

"Are you saying that it was someone else that was following me?"

"It does seem that way. Can you think of anyone else that might want you followed?"

"No, I can't."

"So, if it's not about you and Mr. Mudd blackmailing dear old dad, then why and who would knock off Mudd?"

She started to say something when I interrupted her.

"I'm not asking. I'm just thinking out loud. Maybe Mr. Mudd was into more than we know. If you can think of anything else, give me a call. Better yet, stop by my office."

I left off the conversation with Ms. Carworth and drove back to Maggie's restaurant. The day was wearing down, and I wanted to see how she was making out. I figured I had better get Maggie's Plymouth back to her before it got wrecked.

I wasn't sure now if the threat on Maggie's life was connected to the so-called blackmail or Mudd's murder. Either way, I had to find out what was going on.

When I arrived at the restaurant, the place was full. It looked like Maggie had finally gotten her wish. She was running a Delmonico steak with mashed potatoes and green beans special for supper. It sounded so good that I had to order a plate myself.

I sat down at the counter and told the waitress that I would wait for a booth to open. I never liked eating at the counter. That was for drinking.

Maggie got a free minute and came over and gave me a big hug.

"How you doing, Mr. Detective? The booth in the corner just opened. Do you want to move over there?"

"Sure, and bring me the special with a glass of iced tea."

I moved to the booth and sat down. Maggie brought me my dinner.

"Sit down and talk to me a minute," I said.

"Okay, what do you want to talk about?"

"The person who threatened you—did you recognize the voice?"

"No, not really. It was a very husky voice like they were trying to disguise it or something."

"Do you think you would recognize it if you heard it in normal tones?"

"Maybe. I'm not sure though."

"Well, if you ever hear it or even think you do, get a description of him, okay?"

"Oh, I will; you can be sure of that."

"Good. Now why don't you let Hazel close for you, and we can head home."

"Fine. I'll see if she's free to do that."

Hazel said she would close for Maggie.

We left the restaurant and went to my place. I picked up my old Ford, and we drove to Maggie's place.

Maggie's home was furnished with cheap furniture. Chances were she had to pay for it herself. Her husband at the time wasn't known as a hard worker. The lazy bum really didn't work at all.

The world is full of people like that. I must say my own father was a hardworking man. He always said that if a man doesn't work, neither should he eat. I guess that old saying stuck with me.

Maggie made a pot of coffee and served cake and ice cream. She knew I had a weakness for chocolate cake with vanilla ice cream.

We settled down in the living room to watch television. A Western was playing. The show was called the *Lone Ranger*. It was about an ex-Texas ranger that wore a mask and caught bad guys.

I think Maggie must have spent most of her savings on her Television. Personally, I think they're a waste of time.

After the *Lone Ranger,* the evening news came on with breaking news concerning Maggie's restaurant. We couldn't believe what the newscaster was saying. He was talking about a robbery at the restaurant, and a female was dead. They were saying it was Maggie.

The newscaster was saying that a lone witness was in the restroom when he heard gunfire. He then ran out of the restroom only to see a large man running from the building. He jumped in a black sedan and sped off.

Maggie was speechless. When she was finally able to speak, all she could say was, "That was meant for me."

I didn't want to worry Maggie so I said,

"No, darling. It was just a robbery," I said.

"No it wasn't. I'm sure someone is trying to kill me."

I couldn't help thinking that she might be right, but I didn't want her to know I thought that too. This whole thing was getting bazaar.

I had to take Maggie to the hospital and get her a shot to calm her down. The lady that was shot was her best friend, Hazel. They had been friends since fifth grade.

I decided I would take Maggie somewhere where she would be safe. I drove her to my mother's place. I could tell Mom didn't like the idea too much. She was always saying that I should go back to Shirley. She reluctantly said Maggie could stay for a few days until I could clear this thing up. I told her I wasn't sure how long it would take but I would pick up Maggie as soon as it was over.

It was nearly two thirty in the morning when I left Mom's house. I drove to my apartment to catch a few hours' sleep.

CHAPTER 11

It was a short nap. I woke to a slapping noise in the kitchen. I jumped out of bed and ran to see what was going on.

It was the kitchen window that I had left open all night. The wind had picked up, and it was raining hard.

It was seven thirty in the morning. I decided that I might as well stay up. I needed to get an early start. I wanted to go the channel nine office and see if I couldn't talk to the newscaster that covered the story last night. He owed me a favor.

I pulled him and his fine Packard car out of a ditch one night. He was drunk as a skunk, and I took him to my place until he sobered up. I think he and his employer had words from what he was saying. I guessed they got things straight. He was still working.

I drove to 2900 Wilshire Boulevard where channel nine broadcasted from. I parked in their lot and went inside.

A secretary greeted everyone that came in. She was a beautiful brunette with big brown eyes and a perky smile.

"Can I help you?" she said.

"Maybe. I need to see Owen Clark. Is he available?"

"I believe he's here. Who should I say is calling?"

"Charlie McQuillen. He knows who I am. We're old friends."

"Okay. I'll tell him you're here."

She got up from the desk and wiggled her way through the closed doors. If I didn't know better, I would have thought she was flirting with me. *Oh well, must be my imagination.* I took a seat and waited for Owen.

It didn't take long until he was standing in front of me shaking my hand.

"How you doing, Charlie? It's been a couple months since that incident, hasn't it?"

"I believe so. I was wondering if you could toss me some information about the robbery at the restaurant last night."

"Well, I did find out that the lady that was killed wasn't who we thought she was."

"I know. Her name is Hazel Waters."

"Is she a friend of yours, Charlie?"

"You could say that. She worked for a lady friend of mine."

"Since you know her name, what else is there you want to know?"

"Can you tell me anything about the witness that saw the robbery? What all did he tell you about it?"

"Not much. He said he was in the bathroom and heard a shot and came running out to see a man leaving the scene in a hurry."

"Did he say if he could recognize the car he got away in?"

"At first he said it was a black sedan. Then he said it was a black Hudson.

That revelation startled me. All of a sudden, I realized that this wasn't about a robbery or the blackmail of Mr.

Wortts Senior. It was more involved than that, and I had to make sure Maggie was safe at all cost.

"Say, can you give me the witness's name? I need very much to talk to him. I can tell you that this whole deal is involved with something else I'm working on, and it could be—or I should say it *is*—a matter of life or death concerning someone I like very much."

"Seeing you put it that way, his name is Michael Snow. Remember I never said a thing to you about it. We're supposed to keep his name out of it until the police get done with their investigation."

"I understand. Do you have an address on him?"

He reached in his suit coat pocket and brought out a small notebook.

"Let's see." He started leafing through the pages. "Oh, here it is. He lives at 4833 Danbury Drive in LA."

CHAPTER 12

I thanked Mr. Clark and left in a hurry. I had to get to Maggie really quick.

I drove to my mothers' house and went inside. Mom and Maggie were having morning coffee.

"You girls okay?"

"We're fine," Mom said. "Why?"

I walked over to the kitchen table, pulled out a chair, and sat down.

"Oh, no reason. Just thought I'd ask."

Mom got up and went to the cupboard. She took out a cup and poured me a cup of her strong coffee. I never understood why she made it so strong. Mom and Dad would go out to eat in a restaurant and add instant coffee to the coffee they ordered. They explained that restaurant coffee was always too weak to drink so they put in a spoon full of instant coffee. It's just better that way they would say.

"How about a cup of coffee, Charlie?"

"Sure, put some water in for me."

I leaned over to Maggie.

"I have something I need to tell you, but I don't want to say anything in front of Mom."

"We can go out on the front porch and sit in the porch swing if you want to."

"Okay. We're going out on the porch, Mom. I'll come back in before I leave."

"All right, Charlie. You know I don't get to see much of you anymore don't you?"

"Yes Mom but I promise that I change that from now on."

Maggie and I went out to the porch and sat down on the swing.

"Now what is it that's so important, Charlie?"

"You need to stay here for a few days more while I figure this thing out."

"How long, Charlie? I like your mother, but I don't think she likes me. She's always talking about Shirley."

"I'm sorry about that. She thinks we should have stayed together. I can't get it through to her it was Shirley that called it off. Anyway, I don't want to scare you, but I think you're right about what happened last night. I found out that the witness to the crime said he saw a black Hudson leaving the scene. That's the kind of vehicle that ran me off the road."

"That does scare me, Charlie. What are we going to do?"

"You're going to stay here for a few days, okay?"

"What about my restaurant? Who will run it while I'm gone?"

"You don't have to worry about that. The police have closed the place pending an investigation. They have the place all taped off. No one can get in or out. You'll be safe here. If you get too uncomfortable here, I'll find another place you can stay."

"Fine, Charlie, whatever you say."

I left Maggie in the hands of my mother again and headed for Dewberry Drive where Mr. Snow lived. I wasn't sure what shift he worked or if he worked at all, so I planned on just shadowing his place until I saw him. It was already 3:00 p.m. If he worked days, he would be getting home soon.

I arrived at Danbury Drive about a half hour later. There was a blue Dodge in the driveway. I pulled in behind the Dodge, got out of my car, and walked to the door. I rang the doorbell several times. A middle-aged man answered the door.

"Yes, may I help you?" he asked.

"I hope so. My name is Charlie McQuillen. I'm a private investigator, and I would like to know if you could give me some information about the robbery you witnessed last night."

"I told everything I knew to the police last night. I don't know if I can tell you anything more than what I told them."

"May I come in while we talk?"

"Sure. You'll have to forgive my manners."

The Snows had a quaint little two-bedroom home not quite big enough for a family.

"Just me and my wife, LuAnn, live here now. We had one son that lived with us for twenty-five years before he moved out. LuAnn said she thought he would never move, but he did. Since LuAnn died, I haven't been on top of things."

"I understand. When my wife left me, I was a little rattled for a while. I understand you said that you saw a black Hudson sedan leaving the restaurant in a hurry. Do you know for sure if he was the guy that robbed the place?"

"Well, like I told the police, he was the only person around at the time, and I assumed it was him that did the robbery."

"Can you tell me why you were there at that time last night?"

"Sure. I stop there and eat supper most nights. I work as a guard for the bank just down the block. I work the second shift, and that's the time I eat supper, and I leave when the girls are closing."

"Did you get a good look at the guy?"

"All I can tell you is he was a big guy, about six feet tall. He looked to be pretty muscular."

"So you never saw his face?"

"No, he was running away from me."

"You didn't get a plate number either; I suppose?"

"Like I told the police, it was too dark in the street to see a plate number. I have been saying for months they need to put more lights on that street. Maybe they will listen to me now."

"Don't count on it," I said. "Now you're sure the car you saw was a Hudson?"

"I'm pretty sure. I used to have one just like it. LuAnn didn't like it, so I sold it, and we bought the Studebaker. She liked it much better. Women are strange like that, you know."

"Yes, I do know. Thanks for your time, Mr. Snow."

I took out one of my business cards and handed it to him.

"If you think of anything else, please give me a call. Okay?"

"I will, Mr. McQuillen. I'll be sure to do that."

I left the Snows' place and headed back to Maggie's restaurant. Maybe I could find a few clues the police wouldn't be looking for.

To the cops, it was just a robbery, but I knew better. There were a few apartments above the businesses in the area. Someone else might have seen something.

CHAPTER 13

I arrived at the restaurant. The police still had the place taped off. That was good. Maybe there was still a clue or two around.

I parked the old Ford and walked down the block, being very careful not to disturb anything within the taped area.

I noticed that where the so-called getaway car was parked, some oil had dripped on the asphalt. Could it be from the getaway vehicle? It was worth noting in my little book of clues.

I looked up and down the street. There was only one light on in an apartment, and it was down the street going the other way. Most people were asleep that time of night because most of those people worked in the shops in the daytime. That wet spot on the ground might prove costly to some fool if I ever found that Hudson.

I thought it best that I go to my place and spend the night. I remembered Mr. Johnson might still be following me. I was sure he hadn't followed me to my mother's home, and I didn't want anyone to know where Maggie was staying.

I drove to my apartment, and Mrs. Kates was standing on her porch. I pulled up and stopped. I got out of my car, and Mrs. Kates called me over. I walked up to her porch.

"Mr. McQuillen, there was some guy here looking for you."

"Did he say what he wanted?"

"No, he said that he needed to talk to you, but he wouldn't tell me what it was about."

"Did he give you a name?"

"I asked him his name. He said that it wasn't important—that he would catch you later."

"Do you remember what he looked like?"

"Yes, he was a short, heavyset fellow."

"Okay, I think it was my police friend. I'll see him tomorrow. I'll talk to you later, Mrs. Kates."

I left Mrs. Kates standing on her porch admiring the stars in the sky. I went into my apartment. I made a pot of coffee, turned off the lights, and waited just in case the next visitor wasn't a friendly one.

Two o'clock came, and nothing happened, so I shut my eyes for a few hours' sleep. I knew if there were any noises made, I would wake up. I'm a very light sleeper. War does that to a person.

I woke the next morning, showered, shaved, and took off for downtown. I found myself pulling into police headquarters. I made my way to homicide division. John Gabor was sitting at his desk. He looked up to see me walking through his door.

"Just the guy I want to see," John said.

"Really? I must have ESP. I just started driving and wound up here. What did you want to see me about, John?"

"You know we took a plaster cast of the tire tracks around the scene of the robbery?"

"Yeah, I figured you would. How did that turn out?"

"Well, those tracks matched the ones that we took when Mr. Mudd got himself knocked off. So what I'm saying is it was the same vehicle in both cases."

"I had a hunch that was the case. Too many things weren't adding up right for it to be incidental."

"So do you have anything more about the case you can tell me?" John said.

"Not much. I talked to the witness, and he told me he saw a black Hudson. That's when it hit me that the two cases were related. I believe Maggie is in danger, and I think the guy thought he was plugging her. When he realizes he didn't get her, he'll be back."

"I think you're right. Do you have her in a safe place, or do you think she needs police protection?"

"I have her at my mom's place right now. I think she'll be okay there for a while—that is, if she and my mom can get along."

"Yeah, I know your mother pretty well myself. She's a good mother though."

"I know. She wants to overprotect me since Dad passed on."

"My dad is the same way," John said.

"I think I'll go see if I can find out more about Mr. Mudd. He has to be connected to this thing somehow."

"I believe you're probably right. I do know you had better watch yourself. This guy is very dangerous. When you knock off two people to keep a secret quiet, that tells me he's dangerous."

"I'm sure that the redhead, Ms. Carworth, knows more than she's saying too. I found out she's the daughter of Mr. Wortts Senior, and she was pinching him for money and a fine Caddy to drive. She said that was all there was to the so-called blackmail, and he agreed with her in a separate conversation. I'm not so sure that either one of them is telling me the truth. He wants to get elected to the Senate and wants me to keep quiet about his little indiscretion. That's not my business because I don't get into politics. That's more dangerous than anything else I know."

"Well, keep your eyes open and keep me informed on what's going on. We'll be looking into this in the same way. I believe the two cases are related too. I don't believe the same guy knocked off two people for different reasons either."

CHAPTER 14

I left John with a lot of questions unanswered. He did the same for me. I also had to wonder if maybe Mr. Johnson knew more than he was saying. I hadn't noticed him following me lately. To tell the truth, I had forgotten all about him. Maybe he gave up on the idea that Mr. Wortts thought the blackmail thing was solved. That little story wouldn't keep me from investigating more.

I'd just put some heat up against Huey's head and see what he knew.

I knew Huey wasn't one of the guys in the Buick that picked up the redhead that night from my parking lot. So that meant there were a lot more people involved in this than I figured. That was why I needed to find him and get some answers. I didn't get a good look at the two guys with Ms. Carworth the night I nearly got caught in her house. They both were big like Huey. I thought they were the same two that tried to strong-arm me a couple days later. I might have to put heat up beside their heads too. Someone knew what was going on, and I intended to find out.

I pulled into the parking lot where my office was located. I needed to check in to see if anyone left me a note or something. I walked the five flights of stairs up and found my office door closed with no notes sticking out. I guessed I had no visitors since Huey came by. I unlocked my door and went in and settled down on my very old swivel chair. It squeaked every time I turned around in it. I was down examining where the squeak was when, to my surprise, Mr. Johnson walked in.

"Just the guy I've been wanting to see."

"That's funny. I wanted to see you too."

"What's on your mind, Huey?"

"I wanted to tell you that I no longer work for Mr. Wortts. He told me that the blackmail case was solved and he no longer needed my services. What do you think of that?"

"I think you're probably right because he told me the same thing. He told me all about his not so legitimate daughter. He said that there wasn't any blackmail and I should forget the whole thing. So I am."

"I know I shouldn't be saying anything, but I'm sure there is more to this than what he's saying."

"Why do you say that?"

"Because I heard Mr. Wortts talking to his wife one night. They didn't know I overheard them talking about something that they said couldn't get out, and it wasn't about Ms. Carworth either."

"How do you know that?"

"Because he was saying it was something about what he had done in the army and no one should ever find out."

"So your job was to what? Guard Ms. Carworth?"

"No, I was only to guard Mr. Wortts until he found out it was his own daughter that was putting the squeeze on him. I guess she promised to keep quiet if he set her up with a nice cash flow. He agreed to it. You might want to snoop around and see if you can get a peek at Mr. Wortts's military records."

"Yeah, I may just do that. Who are these two goons that hang around Ms. Carworth? They picked her up in a hurry one night outside of my office."

"They must be Mr. Wortts's private bodyguards. Were they a couple big guys wearing suits, riding a Buick?"

"That sounds like them."

"They do special chores for the whole family, not just the old man."

"So he keeps them on the payroll at all times?"

"Yeah, they're permanent employees."

"Is there anything more you can tell me about the family?"

"I can't think of anything. I have only worked for Mr. Wortts for a couple of months. He figured he needed extra muscle when he thought he was in danger. He paid me a lot of money to keep quiet about who was blackmailing him. I figured since you already knew about it, I might as well tell you the other thing—you know, the army thing."

"That's good, Huey. Don't let anyone know that you told me anything, okay?"

"I got you, Mr. McQuillen. I won't tell anyone anything about what I know. It wouldn't be professional."

"That true. Well, thanks for stopping in. If I need some muscle, I'll give you a call."

"Okay, Mr. McQuillen, but I don't think you could afford me. I get twenty-five bucks an hour when I'm on duty, so I'll have to do it for free."

"You're a great guy, Huey."

"No, I just like you, Mr. McQuillen, but I love women if you know what I mean."

"I know what you mean. You're not a funny fellow."

"That's right. Let me know if you need anything."

"Will do."

Mr. Johnson left my office in a slow walk. It would be hard for a man his size to get in a hurry. I would sure hate to have him connect a punch on my jaw though. He could kill a man.

I got up from my chair and walked to the window. Huey still hadn't made it down to his fine-looking Chrysler convertible. I wasn't sure how much I could trust him. He didn't seem like the kind of person that would shaft you. Still, it wouldn't hurt to keep an eye open and on him.

I decided to follow him down. I had a can of oil in the trunk of my car I could use to oil my chair with. When I arrived at the bottom of the stairs, Mr. Johnson was just getting in his vehicle. I walked outside and went to my car. I raised the trunk lid and reached for the can of oil. A pair of my old army boots lying in the trunk caught my eye. I thought, why not go to the base and see if I could get some info on Mr. Wortts's army life? Too bad Jerry wasn't at work yet. *He could find out all the dope on Mr. Wortts. I'll see if I can talk to Gus. He may be able to find out something for me too.*

I drove to the army base, went to the gate, and told them I needed to see Colonel Gus Harden. They waved me on through. I drove to the building where Gus worked, parked, and went inside. There was a sergeant sitting at the reception desk.

He was a tall, slim man, not too muscular. It didn't look as if he'd done much in the physical training department. I walked to the old desk that he was sitting at. He stared up at me for a few seconds. I noticed the name on his shirt said Henry, which would be a surname. The rank on his sleeve denoted that he was a sergeant.

"Is Gus in, Sergeant?"

"No, sir. May I help you?"

"I don't believe so. When will the colonel be back?"

"Not sure, sir. Are you sure I can't help you?"

"Can you get files of anyone that has served in the army?"

"You mean personnel files? I'm not supposed to get into anything like that. But for a good reason, I may be able to find out something."

"How about fifty bucks?"

"That might do it. Who is the person you want to find out about and why?"

"I need to know about an officer by the name of Jack Wortts. He was a full-bird colonel when he left the service."

"Why do you need information about him?"

"He asked me to inquire into his record to see if there was anything derogatory there that might mess up his chances in the election."

He thought about it for a few seconds.

"Oh, so Mr. Wortts asked you to look into his record."

I lied and said, "That's right. He's running for the Senate, you know, and he doesn't want anything in there that would hurt his chances."

"I'll see what I can find out. You won't tell anyone that I did this for you, will you?"

"Not a soul. My sources—I keep my mouth shut about what they do for me."

"Great. I'll be back in a couple minutes."

The sergeant left his desk and was gone about ten minutes. When he came back, he had a file.

"Here you go. Remember—don't tell anyone about this."

I made a gesture pretending to zip my mouth. He handed me the files, and I sat down to review them.

My search was turning up nothing. It seemed Mr. Wortts was as clean as a newly washed shirt. Maybe Huey misunderstood what they were saying. There was nothing in there but good deeds, so he wouldn't be messed up by anything in his records. I pushed the file toward the sergeant.

"Here you go, Sergeant. Nothing in here that would hurt him."

I reached into my pocket and took out my wallet. I took out a fifty-dollar bill and handed to him. He hurriedly took the fifty and stuck it in his pocket. I said good-bye and left the building. *This was just another dead end, or I'm just not looking in the right place.*

CHAPTER 15

I left the army post and headed to Mom's house. I figured I had better check on the girls to see how they were doing. When I arrived at Mom's, it looked as if there was no one at home. I pulled in the driveway and parked. Mom didn't come to the door. That kind of worried me a little. I walked up and opened the door and went in. Mom was standing at the kitchen sink washing a few dishes.

"Charlie, I didn't come to the door because I think someone is watching the house."

"Why do you think that?"

"There is a man that stands on the corner across from the house. He's been there all day."

I walked over to a window facing the road and looked out. Sure enough, there he was, still standing there.

"He hasn't offered to come to the house, has he?"

"No, he just stands there. I told Maggie to stay out of sight just in case he's looking for her."

"Did you call the police?"

"Do you think I should?"

"I think it might be a good idea."

I picked up the phone and called John Garbor. A gruff voice answered the phone.

"Homicide. Can I help you?"

"Hello, John."

"Yeah, what can I do for you, Charlie?"

"Do you have a plainclothes cop across from Mom's house?"

"As a matter of fact, I do. Is that okay with you? I told him not to look suspicious. I guess he failed to do that."

"Mom has a good eye for things like that."

"I told him not to bother them because I figure they wouldn't open the door for a stranger. He was supposed to stay out of sight. I'm going to have a man there until this thing get solved."

"That may take a long time," I said.

"I hope not. I don't have a big budget for personal guards, you know."

"I know. I may have a friend that I can trust to stay close to them. He said if I needed anything, he would help me out free of charge. So let me know when you have to pull your man out."

"I will."

"I may have to move them both. I can't risk either one of them getting hurt."

"You let something happen to your mama, and I might take care of you myself. I adopted her for my own since my mama died."

"She loves you too, John. I'll give you a call and let you know what I'm going to do with them."

"Okay, bye," John said.

I hung up the phone and turned to Mom.

"Where's Maggie?"

"She's in the bedroom."

I walked into the bedroom. It was still the same as it was when Dad was alive. There was her big four-poster bed that they had when I was a kid. There was a rug on the floor with a flowered pattern. She always kept the curtains closed. She was afraid someone would look in on them at night. She was always paranoid that way. Maggie got up from the bed and hugged me. She started to cry.

"Don't cry, doll. I'll take good care of you."

"Why is someone trying to kill me?"

"They think you know something. Is there anything you can think of that you don't think is important? That could be the secret. Maybe something about the Wortts you may have heard or seen?"

"No, I can't think of anything at all."

"What about when you went with Peter Wortts?"

"I only went with him a couple of months. They never let me get too involved with him. His mother and father forced me to sever our relationship."

"Is it okay with you if I question Mr. Peter Wortts?"

"I guess it would be all right. Like I said, there's nothing there."

"I think you'll be safe here for a few days. The guy across the street is a cop. I'll keep checking on you just to make sure. Where can I find Peter these days?"

"He was kind of a cast out from the rest of the family. I met him at a club downtown. He played piano in the band there. The place was called Nightlife. I assume he's still playing there."

"Okay. I'll check it out tonight."

I checked the phonebook and found the address of the Nightlife nightclub. They were on the corner of Sixth and Grand. That wouldn't be hard to find.

I hung around and had supper with Mom and Maggie. We sat around and talked until nine o'clock. I checked the street and saw John's man was still there. I told Mom and Maggie good night and said I would be back later.

I figured I would go downtown where Mr. Wortts was playing and quiz him about a few things. I wasn't exactly sure what I was going to ask him about. I would have to play it by ear. I went out, got the old Ford started, and drove off. I didn't acknowledge John's man standing there. I didn't want to bring any undue attention to him, just in case someone was watching.

It was a clear night with a full moon. It would be easy to tail someone. Too bad I didn't have someone to follow. I sped of down the street, turned the corner, and pulled into a driveway, watching to see if anyone was following me. No one passed by, so I guessed nobody tailing me.

It took me about thirty minutes to get to the club. The band was still playing. I found a seat at a table and sat down. The waitress came over to take my order.

"May I get you something, sir?"

"Bring me a me a scotch and ginger." That's all I would have to drink. "Is that Peter Wortts on the piano?"

"Yes, sir. He's been playing here a long time. Why?"

"I want to buy him a drink."

"Okay. I'll take it to him."

"Great. Could you tell him I would like to talk to him?"

"Sure."

The waitress took Peter a margarita and told him I wanted to talk to him. She brought my drink to me.

"Is that what he always drinks?"

"Yep, as long as I've been here. Why?"

"No reason. Just wondered."

The band played another ten minutes then took a break. Peter walked over to my table and introduced himself.

"Peter Wortts here. I think you already know that, don't you? If you're here on my father's behalf, you can forget it."

"No, my name is Charlie McQuillen. I'm a Private Investigator and it's about another matter."

"What could that be? I don't do anything but play piano and aggravate my dear old dad."

"How come you didn't follow in the family tradition like your brother?"

"That's their life, not mine. I can't stand the hypocrisy. I feel clean playing my piano."

"It doesn't pay too well, does it?"

"It ain't always about the money now, is it?"

"That's true. You used to go with a girl named Maggie Hecktor, right?"

"Sure. So what?"

"Do you know any reason why your family might want to hurt her?"

"No. I didn't go with her long enough for her to find out anything about us."

"Did she know about Ms. Carworth?"

When I asked that question, I realized I might have opened a can of worms that wasn't supposed to be opened. I remembered Ms. Carworth saying the other family members didn't know anything about the man's illegitimate child, and I might have let the cat out of the bag.

"What about Leslie?"

"Nothing. I spoke out of turn."

"Don't worry about it. I have an idea that Leslie is most likely our half sister. Either that or she's the old man's sweet thing, and no, I don't believe she knew anything about Leslie."

"Do you know anything about James Mudd?"

101

"Only that Leslie used to go with him, and he got to annoying her at the end. That is, before he was killed. I don't think she would kill him for that."

"I don't either. Do you know why they broke up?"

"Not really. She never talked about her love life at all. I'm not sure if she was seeing anyone else or not. There was another army guy with them one day when they stopped by the old man's house, but I don't think there was anything romantic about it. What I mean is they weren't competing for her hand, so to speak."

"You wouldn't happen to know his name, would you?"

"No, the two of them sat in the car while Leslie came in the house to talk to my father."

"What about that conversation? Did you hear any of it?"

"Sorry, no."

"Do you think your brother Jack would talk to me about it?"

"Sure, for the right price, he'll talk to anyone."

"I had a free conversation in mind."

"Maybe. You could try. Do you know where his office is?"

"As a matter of fact, I have never been there before."

"Hey, look, man, it's time I get on stage. If you want to talk again, just stop by and buy me a drink. I come cheap."

"Thanks for the help. Maybe we'll talk again," I said.

He raised his glass then got up and walked to the stage.

I sat and listened to the music for a while. Peter Wortts was a pretty good piano man. I always wished I could play music. *I guess I have to settle for shaking my tambourine. Oh well, that's life.*

It was about ten thirty. I decided to take the long way to Mom's just in case I picked up a tail somewhere.

CHAPTER 16

The lights were still on when I got to Mom's place. John's man was still on the corner in his unmarked car. Didn't look as if anything went on while I was gone.

I parked in the driveway and went inside. Mom and Maggie were at the table having coffee. I got a cup from the cupboard and poured myself some of Mom's coffee. I sat down at the table.

"Did you find out anything?" Maggie asked.

"I'm not sure. I found out that James Mudd visited Mr. Wortts's home one night with Leslie and anther army person. You wouldn't happen to remember anything like that, would you?"

"My goodness, that was a few months ago, but I do remember I was there one night with Peter when Leslie came in and wanted to talk to Mr. Wortts. Mr. Wortts asked her where James was, and she said he was in the car with someone she called … what was that name? I can't recall now."

"I wish you could; that may be the connection to you."

"Do you think he might have something to do with the murder of James Mudd?"

"It's the only thing I have right now. Unfortunately, James is dead, and he can't talk to me. It's possible that other person thinks you might remember him."

"He could be right too. Leslie did mention his name to me and Peter. I just don't recall what it was. I do remember she said he was a major in the army."

"Maybe I'll go snoop around at the army post tomorrow and see if there's anyone that might know who that officer was. Maybe Gus could help me with that."

It was already eleven thirty. Mom didn't usually stay up too late at night. Her and Dad believed in getting a good night's sleep. I don't know how I got so messed up. I never go to bed before two. Most times.

"Charlie, you can sleep in the bedroom on the left. There are clean sheets on the bed. Maggie can sleep with me."

Mom had another rule. You had to be married if you planned on sleeping together in her house. That came from old southern Christian teaching. Her and Dad lived by the Bible as long as I could remember.

"Okay, Mom, you know I know your rules."

Mom went to her bedroom. Maggie stayed behind.

"I'll be there in a minute, Mrs. McQuillen."

"Okay. I'll leave the light on."

Maggie and I went to the sofa and had a seat. I couldn't stand it any longer. Sitting there looking at how beautiful she was. I reached and pulled her over to me, and we engaged in hot, passionate kissing for about five minutes. I never realized how much I missed her until then. She always smelled like fresh spring and felt just as good.

"Charlie, I hope you find who's doing this real soon. I'm scared to death."

"I think I'm closing in on the person who's responsible."

I had to tell Maggie something positive so she would feel better.

"I guess we better not get too involved. I don't want your mother to come out and see something she shouldn't."

"Believe me, I don't either.

I picked myself up and offered Maggie my hand. Maggie stood, and I walked her to the bedroom. We kissed and parted.

I went back to the kitchen and emptied the coffee pot. Then I sat down at the table to reflect on what all I had learned. I knew I had to go see Jerry again. I just hoped he would wake up soon and have some information on who tried to kill him. With comas, you never know how long they'll last. I was just thankful that Jerry didn't die that night.

It was a warm night. I knew I wouldn't be able to sleep in the bedroom. I got a pillow from the bedroom and lay down on the sofa. I figured it would be better just in case someone might get to John's man outside and then try for us. We were dealing with a vicious killer that could snuff someone out without thinking about it.

Seven o'clock came, and Mom was up. The air in the house was warm and stale because the women didn't want me to raise the windows. It was daylight now, so I went around raising them. John's man was still there on the corner, looking a little beat. I didn't worry so much in daylight as long as there was one of LA's finest on the job. I'd leave Maggie there as long as I could. Mom and her seemed to be getting along okay. Maybe Mom decided that Shirley and I were really over and Maggie was a great person.

Mom was in the kitchen making breakfast. Maggie was in the bathroom taking a shower. I don't remember ever seeing Maggie dirty. She is one of those clean freaks you hear about.

I sat at the table, and Mom put a plate of ham and eggs in front of me. She knew my favorite foods.

Maggie finished and came out and sat down at the table with me. Mom put a plate of ham and eggs down for Maggie. She always figured people should eat what they're served when you're in someone's home. Maggie got up and got me and her a cup of coffee.

We were having a good talk at breakfast when the phone rang. Mom answered. It was John Gabor.

Mom handed me the phone.

"Hello, John. What's up?"

"Got some good news for you. Your friend Jerry is out of his coma."

"Is he okay?"

"Yes, they just called me from the hospital. He didn't know where he was, but he could talk."

"Did he say anything about what happened?"

"No, he's a little fuzzy on that. I thought you might want to know he came out of the coma."

"I sure did, thanks. Can I go see him?"

"Sure. I'll let my man know you're coming so he won't try to stop you from going in."

"Great. I appreciate that more than you know, John."

"No problem. You'll keep me informed on what you find out, I take it?"

"You know I will. I'll see you later and fill you in."

"Okay, bye."

I hung up the phone. I turned to Mom and Maggie sitting at the table.

"I guess you heard—Jerry's okay."

"That's great, honey," Mom said.

"Do you think Jerry has anything he can tell you about this case?" Maggie said.

"I'm guessing he knows something. Whether he remembers it or not is another matter. I'm going to take a shower and go see him today."

I finished my breakfast, took a shower, kissed the girls good-bye, and headed to the hospital.

I parked in the lot and went to the reception desk. There was a bright-eyed lady at the desk.

"May I help you?"

"I would like to see Jerry Williams."

She retrieved a card from the file.

"What is your name?"

"Charlie McQuillen," I said.

"Okay, you can go up. Do you know where he's at?"

"I'm not sure. He was in intensive care."

"They moved him to room 312. You can go right up."

"Thank you."

She handed me a pass card, and I headed for the elevator.

There were two ladies on the elevator crying. I guess they had a tragedy of their own to deal with. I acknowledged them but said nothing. We arrived at the third floor. I excused myself and left the elevator. The two ladies stayed on and went up. I assumed they had someone in intensive care.

I found room 312 and went in. Jerry was sitting up trying to eat. He was sure looking pale and tired. That was the first solid food he had in days. Jerry looked up at me.

"I remember you, Charlie, but I don't remember much about how I got here."

"Someone tried to kill you. You wound up in a ditch with a bullet in you. John has been keeping a guard on your room ever since."

"Remind me to thank him."

"I will. Do you remember anything about that night?"

"Not much. Everything is still just a blur. I do remember seeing a dark sedan trying to pass me when the lights went out."

"Could it have been a black Hudson?" I said.

"It could have been. The more I think about it, I think it was a Hudson. Why? Is that important?"

"It was a guy in a Hudson that ran me down, and the same vehicle was seen at another crime. So, yes, I believe it is important. Make sure you stay on guard. I think the same guy is out to get you. I got a couple leads I'm going to check out at the base. I'm going to talk to Gus and see if he knows anything more about James Mudd."

"Do you think he had something to do with all of this?"

"Do you remember anything about Mudd?"

"I remember he was in the same building, but I can't remember if he was in the same office. A few things are beginning to come back to me."

"That's good. Maybe everything will come back to you real soon."

"Gus may be able to find out more about Mudd for you than I could."

"Yeah, you could be right. That's why I'm going to visit him when I leave here."

"Gus is a good man. If he can help you, he will," Jerry said.

"Well, take it easy, pal. Let me know when they turn you loose, and I'll come get you."

I left the hospital and headed for the army post. I was glad Jerry was out of danger medically. I still had to worry about who was trying to get him. This created a problem as to where I could hide him until he got better. He was still very vulnerable, and I was sure the killer knew that.

If I could find that Hudson, I could solve this thing. I hadn't seen even one since everything happened. I figured that should work the same as how when you buy a car, you see dozens of them the next day. Seems it never works like that when you need it to.

It was nice and sunny for Los Angeles. It wasn't too hot or too cold. The heat off the old Ford engine kept the inside of the car warm without running the heater.

I drove to the post and stopped at the gate. The guard came out and waved me to stop, which I already knew to do. All the guards knew who I was. It was just a formality for the guards to come out and wave me down.

"Who do you need to see this time, Charlie?"

"I need to see Gus Harden."

"Okay, you know where to go. Have a nice day."

"You have one too, Mitch. See you on the way out."

I drove to the building where Gus worked. I parked in the lot and walked inside. Sergeant Henry was at work at his desk. He looked up and stopped typing as soon as he saw me.

"Can I help you again, sir?"

"Just call me Charlie. Everyone else around here does."

"I haven't been here too long, Charlie. I just transferred here a few weeks ago."

"Is Gus around?"

"No, you're out of luck again. He just stepped out a few minutes ago. I'm sure he won't be back for a couple hours."

"Do you know where he went?"

"He said he had to go to town and would be back later."

"Were you here when Captain James Mudd worked here?"

"James Mudd ... the name does sound familiar. Oh I remember now. He was the guy that bought the farm. He gave his life for that small piece of real estate."

"That's the guy. Did you know much about him?"

"I knew he had the hots for some women that didn't feel the same way."

"How did you know that?"

"We went out for drinks after work one night, and he kept trying to call someone he called Leslie."

"Yeah, I know about her. What about anyone else? Did he have any other friends that you know of?"

"There was another guy that he used to drink with, but he was transferred to another post. He left the same day that Mudd was killed."

"Do you know his name?"

The sergeant rubbed his head in deep thought.

"I believe his name was Captain Fredrick Wonderful. Actually it was spelled Wodervull. They seemed to be good friends too. Mudd was always talking about what a great guy Wodervull was."

"Do you think he was good for the murder?"

"That I wouldn't know. I'm a bad judge of what people might do."

"Do you think you could find out where he was transferred to?"

"Sure, I could check the files. You did say this is for a good cause, didn't you?"

"You bet it is. I'm trying to solve Captain Mudd's murder and hopefully stop a couple people from getting knocked off—that being my best friend and my best girl."

Sergeant Henry got up from his desk and went in the other room. He was gone five minutes then came back with a file. He was reading the file.

"It looks like he was sent to White Sands proving ground near Alamogordo, New Mexico."

"Is it a permanent move?"

"It looks like it."

"Does it say if he flew or drove?"

"I believe he took a flight out the evening of the fifteenth of December."

"Do you think he had time to knock off Mudd then make it to the airport?"

"I guess it's possible, but I wouldn't bet on it."

"I think you're right. It's possible. I may have to go to Colorado and talk to Wonder boy."

"Let me know what you find out. You have my curiosity going full speed now."

I reached in my pocket and pulled out a ten-dollar bill and handed it to Sergeant Henry. He handed it back to me.

"This one is on the house. You did say it was for a good cause, and that's good enough for me."

"Thank you, Sergeant. By the way, what is your first name?"

"Norman, sir. Norman E. Henry."

"Well, thanks for the info. I'll let you know how everything turns out."

I left the army post thinking I would have to make a trip to Alamogordo and get Captain Wodervull's version of what he did that day. I didn't know if I would try to drive the distance or if I should catch a flight. If I could fly, I would have to find a way around the post when I got there. That might be costlier than just driving my car there. I was sure the old Ford would make the trip, but it could be cool there that time of the year.

What the hell. I'll just fly. When I get there, I'll call the captain and see if he'll meet me somewhere to talk.

I drove home and packed a change of clothing. I called the airport and found there was a plane leaving in a couple hours.

CHAPTER 17

I made it to the airport just in time to catch the flight to Alamogordo. I would be flying in a Douglas aircraft DC-3. They were very reliable during World War Two. They left the windows out for the army and called them a C47. They used them to haul military cargo.

Didn't matter what they did to them; they were still loud and noisy and rattled when you took off.

I was taking a chance that the captain was still there, but I didn't have time to check it out before I left.

About three hour later, we were landing at Alamogordo. I deplaned and went inside the terminal. I found a telephone and looked up the base number. I called the base, and they patched me through to Captain Wodervull.

"Captain Wodervull. May I help you?"

"Yes, Captain, my name is Charlie McQuillen. I need to talk to you about the time you spent in Los Angeles."

"Why would you need to talk to me about that? I wasn't there very long until they transferred me here. Is this about a military problem?"

"You could say that. I'd like to talk to you about James Mudd, but I don't want to discuss it over the telephone."

"Okay, there's a restaurant called the Post Time near White Sands. I'll meet you there in about an hour. We can talk there."

"Okay, I'll see you there. Thank you."

I didn't know what to expect, so I brought along some heat just in case he got belligerent. This guy could very well be Mudd's killer. *But what about Hazel's murder" If they're connected, he must have access to flights whenever he needs one or he's working with someone in LA.*

I went to baggage pickup and found my bag. There was always a cab standing by outside. I would get a cab to the restaurant and wait there for Captain Wodervull.

By the time I got to the restaurant, I had about fifteen minutes to kill. I had to go over how I was going to approach the captain. There was always the possibility that he knew nothing at all. Time would tell.

I found a booth and had a seat. The restaurant was nice and clean. I guess to serve military people you have to run a clean joint. The military is real touchy about cleanliness. I would have bet there wasn't any dust on the beams that crossed the ceiling. The tables were made of rough lumber that was sanded real smooth so no one would get a splinter. The lights hung down about ten feet from the ceiling and glowed in a low fashion. The waitress came over and handed me a menu.

"Can I get you something to drink, sir?"

"Just coffee and a glass of water."

She left for the kitchen. It wasn't long until she was back with my order.

"Would you like to order now, sir?"

"Not right now. I'm waiting for someone to arrive. If someone asks for Charlie McQuillen, send them my way."

I sat about ten minutes, and Captain Wodervull walked in. He went to the counter and said something to the waitress. She pointed toward me. I waved my hand at him. He acknowledged. He walked over and sat down.

"Mr. McQuillen, I presume."

"Yes, and you're Captain Wodervull?"

"That's right. What can I do for you? You wanted to tell me or ask me something about James Mudd."

I didn't know how else to say it, so I just came out with it.

"Yes, do you know he got himself knocked off the same day you left Los Angeles?"

I could tell the news had totally rocked his boat.

The waitress started to walk over to our table when I motioned for her not to.

"What do you mean he's dead?"

"Just what I said. He was found just outside Maggie's restaurant on December 15. They said he was with someone that day just before he got shot."

"Shot? Why would someone want to shoot James?"

"I don't know. I thought maybe you might have a clue. How long have you known Captain Mudd?"

"I've known him all my life. We grew up together in Columbus, Ohio. Besides that, he was my cousin."

"Your cousin. That's a twist I hadn't counted on."

"Yes, my cousin and I lived only two houses apart. We even joined the army together. We were always together until we were separated in the war."

"You had no clue that your cousin was dead?"

"No, I haven't heard from him since I arrived here. He had no parents. They were killed in a car crash after high school. It was very hard on him. I thought he would never get over it. I guess he doesn't have to now, does he."

"So there was no bad feeling between you?"

"None. We were closer than brothers. We were always together growing up."

"What about your parents? Are they still alive?"

"Yes, they are. They still live in Ohio. Feel free to talk to them if you like."

"So you don't think they know about James's death?"

"I'm sure they don't or they would have let me know about it."

As I sat studying his face, I was pretty sure he knew nothing about Mudd's death. You learn to read people, and he was reading innocent.

"Do you know if he had other friends in the service that he went to supper or drinks with?"

"I'm sure he had other friends, but I never had the chance to meet any of them."

"Maybe you can clear up something for me."

"If I can."

"Did you know his girlfriend, Ms. Carworth?"

"I never really knew her, but I heard him talk about her on occasion. Most of the time, he didn't have anything pleasant to say about her."

"Did you ever go with him to Jack Wortts's house?"

"No, like I said, I never really met her."

I thought to myself, *This could be like looking for a needle in a haystack. It's hard to tell who this guy was that went to Mr. Wortts's home that night with Leslie.*

I noticed the restaurant served liquor.

"Would you like to order a drink or something?"

"No, not now. I'm going to go home and call my parents and let them know what you told me. Do you know what they did with him?"

"He's probably in the military morgue unless they found a family member to take care of him."

"Can I ask you another question?"

"Sure, I have nothing to hide. Shoot.

"My friend Jerry Williams was working on something for me just before he was shot. There was a military vehicle parked outside Mr. Wortts Sr.'s home one night, either waiting for someone or they were watching the house. Do you know anything about that?"

"What night was it? Do you remember?"

"It was the first week of December."

"I guess I could clear that up for you. I was there with James. He went there to see Leslie. We were only there for about an hour to an hour and a half. I sat in the car while he was inside. The mud was there because I hadn't washed the vehicle yet."

"How long had the mud been there?"

"Just that day. I had been out investigating some undeveloped property the army has and got into some mud. I guess the spinning of the wheels must have slung mud on the plate."

"That sounds reasonable. So that was just an innocent visit that time?"

"I believe so. Like I said, I sat in the vehicle while he was inside. So I have no way of knowing what was said."

"I know you were in the car for a while because I happened to see you that night."

I took one of my business cards out of my jacket pocket and handed it to him.

"If you think of anything more, you'll be sure to call me, right?"

"I sure will. Who are you working for now?"

"Right now, I have no client."

"Can I hire you to look into James's murder? I want the person responsible caught and brought to trial."

I thought for a couple seconds, then decided that I was in the investigating business and there was no reason why I couldn't work for him.

"I suppose I could work for you."

"I'll pay you any amount you want. Just find James's killer."

I thought some more about how much I should charge him. A fellow army man, I didn't want to hit him too hard.

"How about thirty bucks a day and expenses?"

"That sounds reasonable. My parents have money, and I'm sure they would like to know who did this cowardly thing."

"Okay, it's settled then."

He reached in his pocket, pulled out a checkbook, and started to write.

"Will two hundred be enough?"

"That will be just fine."

So far I had made $750 on the deal. He finished writing the check and handed it to me.

"You can fill in your own name, Mr. …"

"Charlie McQuillen," I said.

I shoved the check into my pocket and waved over the waitress. She came over.

"May I help you?"

"Bring me a ham on rye and whatever the captain wants."

"Oh, I don't want anything. I'm just going to go home. You'll keep me informed on what you find out?"

"That I will do," I said.

Captain Wodervull got up, excused himself, and left the building.

"I guess I'll have to eat alone tonight," I said.

"What? A guy like you doesn't have a steady girl?"

"Sure I do. I'm from out of town."

I figured I should stop this before it got started.

"I have a favorite girl back in LA. Say, is there a decent motel around here where a guy could get some rest for the night?"

"There's the Captain's Quarters just down the street about a block. It's real nice. All the service people stay there when they're in town."

"Okay, Captain's Quarters it is. Thanks."

I finished my sandwich and drank a pot of their fine coffee, then walked down the street to the motel.

If the motel was anything like the restaurant, then it would be clean too. I could tell the place hadn't been there too long. I guessed they built it when the army opened White Springs.

White Springs was built to test missiles and nuclear bombs.

So the place was very hush-hush.

I walked into the lobby. The floor had plush red carpet and was decorated with red velvet chairs in various places. *I hope this place fits my budget.* I walked to the counter.

"Would you like a room, sir?"

"How much is a room here?"

"Only ten dollars a night."

"I can handle that. Give me a single room, the one night."

"Yes, sir. I'll put you in room 112. How would that be? It's on the bottom floor."

"That's fine.

I took out a ten spot and handed it to the clerk. He put it in the register and handed me a receipt and a key.

"We have a lounge through those doors if you would like a drink, sir."

"I may just check that out later."

"The band Nightlife plays tonight on stage if you're interested."

"I definitely will check that out."

I couldn't resist live music. I just wished I could play.

I went to my room and settled in. I took a shower and went to the lounge. I thought one little drink wouldn't hurt me. After all, I'm no alcoholic. I spent a couple hours listening to a pretty good band. They played a lot of Western music.

I nursed one drink then retired to my room to get some shuteye.

By eight o'clock, I was up and dressed and heading to the bank where Captain Wodervull had his account. I cashed the check he gave me. I would rather go back to Los Angeles with cash in my pocket than a check. I then headed for the airport and caught the morning flight back home.

CHAPTER 18

LA was warm and smoggy with a little threat of rain in the air. Oh, how I hated the weather when it was like that. It was very hard on my arthritis. My hands got all stiff. I hoped I wouldn't have to use my revolver. It could be tough getting to it.

I found my old Ford in the parking lot and headed for the police station. I told John I would keep him up to date on what I found out. He might have something new for me too.

When I arrived at the police station, I went to John's office. John was staring at his desk, not paying attention to anything.

"Deep in thought, are you?"

"Not really. This case has got me buffaloed. I thought we found your Hudson, but it turned out to be a little old lady on a trip to see her son."

"I had another dead end also. My investigation led me to White Springs, New Mexico, but turned up nothing there. The suspect turned out to be his cousin."

"Too bad the district attorney is pressing me to solve these two murders."

"I'm going to go visit the redhead again. I want to know who the guy was that waited in the car while she talked to old man Wortts on a certain night."

"So you think the redhead knows more than she's saying, huh?"

"There's something suspicious about her involvement in it. I'm going to find Maggie and see if she remembered who the redhead said the guy was. Ms. Carworth had mentioned the guy's name when she was there one evening with Peter Wortts. Maggie went with Peter for a couple months before she met me. When she started seeing me, it was all over for dear old Peter. He may have had nothing to do with it, but right now I'm grabbing at straws."

"Believe me, I know what you mean. Let me know what you find out."

"I will. I'll see you later, John."

John nodded, and I left him to his deep thought.

I drove over to the law office of Jack Wortts Junior. I wanted to talk to him also. Maybe he knew who the guy might be.

I parked in the lot and went up to his office. His secretary was still busy at work on something. She looked up from her typing.

"Are you here to see Leslie again?"

"Not this time, doll. I need to talk to your boss.

"Mr. Wortts?"

"That's the guy, unless you work for someone else."

"Oh no, he's my boss. I'll see if he'll see you. Have a seat. I'll just be a minute."

She gave me a big sexy grin and walked into Wortts's office.

She came back out smiling like she was when she went in.

"He'll see you now."

I laid the magazine down that I had pick up and pretended to read. Sometimes it's better to let them think you're not paying any attention to things at hand. Maybe they'll spill some beans on the floor unintentionally. You know what I mean.

"Thank you," I said.

I walked through the opened doors into the big guy's office.

"Have a seat."

I sat down in another expensive chair. Jack's office was somewhat different from his father's. He had more expensive furniture and drapes that I bet cost five hundred bucks to hang.

"Thank you," I said. "I won't beat around the bush. I know you're a busy man. I talked to your brother Peter, and he says you and him think that Ms. Carworth is your half-sister."

"Sometimes I think Peter talks too much about things he doesn't know much about."

"Don't sell your brother short. He may know more than you think."

"What is it you want to know about?"

"Leslie Carworth."

"My secretary?"

"Do you know where she came from?"

"Sure, she said she came from England. Why?"

"Do you know who she is?"

"She said she was born in England and lived with her mother and stepfather."

"Do you know why your father wanted you to hire her?"

"Yes, he told me that she needed a job, and he had nothing open at the time. He asked me if I could make a place for her. She needed a job to maintain her working status in the United States or she wouldn't be able to get her green card extended."

"Peter tells me that he thinks she's a sister to you and him."

"I know. He's said the same to me, but I have trouble believing that. I don't believe my father would have done that to my mother."

"Why not?" I said.

"Because he's an upstanding and honest man."

"Would you believe me if I told you that Ms. Carworth told me the same thing?"

Jack sat there with a bewildered look on his face, not knowing whether to believe me or not.

"Is that what she told you?"

"As a matter of fact, it is. She has a birth certificate naming your father as the birth parent."

"Even if it's true, what does that have to do with anything?"

"I guess I just wanted to know if you would lie for Leslie or not."

"I can tell you really quick that I wouldn't."

"Okay then, do you know anything about her social life?"

"Do you mean who are her friends? I only know that she used to go with the guy that got himself killed."

"You knew James Mudd?"

"No, I didn't, and at the time he was killed, I was in a meeting here in my office with some clients. Besides, I wouldn't have any reason to kill him."

"Do you know if he was in on the blackmail or not?"

He looked totally surprised when I mentioned blackmail.

"Whose blackmail? There's no one blackmailing me about anything."

"Your father's blackmail. So you knew nothing about your father being blackmailed?"

"I assure you, sir, I knew nothing of the sort. I do intend to find out now though."

"Well, I do believe you are telling the truth," I said. "I have a couple more questions if you don't mind. Do you know any of Leslie's friends that were or are in the military other than James Mudd?"

"I was at my father's home one evening when Leslie and James came to see my father. I didn't want to seem nosey, so I walked over to the window and saw a man sitting in the car they had come in. I can tell you he was a big man, but I couldn't tell you who he was. Like I said, I didn't want to seem nosey, so I never asked about him. I just assumed he was a friend of Leslie's."

"That leaves Captain Wodervull out of the picture."

"What's that?" he said.

"I found out that James had a cousin in the service here too, and his name is Wodervull."

"Oh yes, I know him, and he wasn't the man I saw that night in the car."

"That's good. He hired me to find out who the killer is. I believe I can rule his cousin out as the murderer. Don't you?"

"I don't think he's the man you're looking for either."

"Why is that?"

"Because I understand they were very close—unless it was a jealousy thing. Maybe he wanted Leslie for himself. As you know, she's a very beautiful woman. I still don't think it was that either. He didn't seem interested in her when he was here, but looks can be deceiving."

"Boy, I know that's true. Where is Leslie now? I thought she would be at work."

"She asked me for a few days off. She said it was important, so I said okay."

"Did she say why she needed time off?"

"She didn't say, and I didn't ask."

"I thank you for your time, sir."

"I hope I helped you in some way. I hope you find out who did this terrible thing. I think James was a good man."

"The same person may be guilty of another murder. Plus, an attempt on my fiancée's life."

"I wish you luck, and if there is anything more I can help you with, just let me know."

"I'll do that. Good day to you."

I walked out of Jack's office, and his secretary was still smiling at me as I passed by. I nodded and kept walking.

I retrieved my old Ford and started to drive. I wound up driving along Malibu beach with heavy thoughts on my mind.

I don't think Jack Jr. had anything to do with the murder, nor do I think that Captain Wodervull had anything to do with it. However, Ms. Carworth, as far as I'm concerned, still isn't in the clear. I have to find her and press her a little harder.

The more I thought, the farther up the beach I drove. I found myself north about fifty miles. I figured I had better turn around and head back to town.

CHAPTER 19

I drove into town and stopped at Blackie's bar. I hadn't seen him in a few days. I wanted to see if he had picked up anything through the grapevine. You would be surprised what people brag about in beer joints.

I parked on the street and walked into the bar. Blackie was busy putting ice in their containers. A lot of people like their liquor on ice. Blackie had a cigarette hanging from his mouth. I don't think I ever saw him without one.

"Don't you know those things will kill you?"

"I know, but you have to die from something, don't you?"

"That's true. I decided it wouldn't be a cigarette though. I might get killed by a jealous husband but not a cigarette."

Blackie's bar was dark, and he always had a few drunks sitting at the counter. I refuse to let myself wind up like that. I believe there is more to life than seeing how much alcohol you can pour in your body.

"Well, what are we drinking?"

"Just give me a ginger ale."

"I saw you friend in here again," Blackie said.

"You mean Ms. Carworth?"

"Yeah, she's the redheaded woman you talked to here that night, right?"

"Right. Was she alone?"

"She was for a while. Then a man came in and met with her."

"Did you recognize him?"

"Yeah, he was the guy that was with you the last night you were here. He drank beer, and she drank water.

"Do you mean Jerry?"

"No, the other guy."

"Gus, that's his name. Are you sure it was him?"

"I'm real sure. I was as close to him as I'm to you right now."

"Do you know what they talked about?"

"Not really. I thought they were friends. They both knew the captain that got rubbed. Didn't they?"

"I guess you're right. They could know each other, being they both were friends with Captain Mudd. I guess I'm grabbing at straws trying to solve these murders."

"Yeah, I heard about Hazel getting killed in a robbery. Usually I pick up a few things from the street, but I've heard nothing about that."

"Do you know anyone that drives a Hudson car?"

Blackie shook his head, stating he didn't.

"The guy that was here with the redhead rode a motorcycle. I've never seen him in a car."

"Oh well, I need a new plan of attack. The trail is getting cold, and unless I get lucky, I may not find who is responsible."

"Don't worry about it, Charlie. The guy will make a mistake, and you'll nab him."

"I hope you're right because I got Maggie hid, and now I'm going to have to find a place for Jerry. I think they both could be in danger."

"Do you have a place for Jerry to stay?"

"Not yet. They still haven't released him from the hospital."

"He can stay at my place. I'm here at the bar most of the time, so I wouldn't be in his way."

"That's great. I'll see what he thinks of that idea."

While I was sitting there jawing with Blackie, Gus walked through the door. He walked over to where I was sitting and stopped.

"What's going on, Charlie?"

"Not much. How about you?"

"Same old crap. Are you still looking into James Mudd's murder? Give me a beer, Blackie. Let's have a seat at that booth and talk about it," Gus said.

Blackie handed him a beer, and we retreated to the nearest booth and had a seat.

"As a matter of fact, I am. Have you heard anything more about it?" I said.

"All I've heard is what you hear on the radio. I get it they're looking for a black Hudson."

"Yeah, that same car was at the scene of both murders. Do you know somebody that drives one?"

"I told the cops they should check out that cousin of his. I'm not sure, but he may have been driving one like that."

"I talked to him, and he never mentioned he even had a vehicle other than a military one to drive."

"Well if he had one, he could have gotten rid of it."

"I don't think so. As far I know, he was in New Mexico when Hazel was killed and at the airport when James Mudd was killed."

"Couldn't he have killed him and then made it for the airport?"

"Not enough time. He was due to lift off about the time the murder happened."

"Maybe he faked a flight to New Mexico. Have you thought about that?"

"Now that you put it that way, I guess I didn't think about that. I just took his word for it."

All of a sudden, Gus had a good point.

"I don't mean to tell you your business, but you have to check out everything."

"You're right … you are right. I guess I had better make sure he told me the truth. I'll check that out the first thing tomorrow. I guess I had better ask you where you were that day at that time."

"Hell, that's too long ago for me to remember. Besides, I had no reason to kill him."

"I know, Gus. I'm just pulling your chain."

Gus started to get a little nervous when I asked him where he was at the time of the murder. Maybe I should investigate Gus also.

"Where is Maggie now? I noticed the restaurant is still closed," Gus said.

All of a sudden, I didn't want to trust anyone where Maggie was concerned.

"I got her where she'll be safe until this is over."

"Have you talked to Shirley lately?"

"No, I didn't know you knew Shirley, Gus."

Gus seemed to be digging himself a hole he didn't want to be in.

"Don't you remember? You introduced us one time when the two of you met here one evening."

I didn't want Gus to know, but I didn't remember anything like that happening. I decided to go along with him to save aggravation.

"That was a while back also. I guess you're not the only one with a bad memory."

"The older you get, the worse it gets. Hey look, Charlie, I have to get out of here. Five o'clock comes early, you know."

Gus poured his beer down his throat and got up and left the bar. All of a sudden, I had more questions to get answered. Maybe Gus was just trying to be helpful. Anyway, it wouldn't hurt to check Captain Wodervull's alibi a little further.

I got up from the booth and walked back to the bar and had a seat.

Blackie was busy serving other customers. When he finished, he walked back to where I was sitting.

"Did you learn anything new, Charlie?"

"Not much. However, I did manage to make Gus a little nervous. I think he got the impression that I suspected him in this thing."

"Are you sure he's not involved?"

"I don't think he knew anything about the blackmail. That was just a jilted daughter wanting revenge. That has been all cleared up now."

I sat around talking with Blackie for an hour, and then I left for Mom's place.

CHAPTER 20

The next morning, I got up and chatted with Mom and Maggie.

Maggie told me she loved my mom, but it was tough hearing her talk about Shirley all the time. "She goes on and on all day about how good Shirley was to her," Maggie told me. I reminded Maggie that my mother was just playing mom and not to worry about it.

It seems I will have no choice but to find another place to put Maggie for a while. I can't take her to her folks' home. That would be the first place the killer would look. The only other place I could think to leave her was with Shirley.

Wouldn't that be ironic? An ex-wife and a girlfriend living in the same house together. Stranger things have happened. Besides, if the killer knew that Maggie and I were seeing each other, chances were he wouldn't think of her being with Shirley.

Okay, I thought. *I'll call Shirley and see if Maggie can stay with her for a few days.*

Since the girls went to the local market, it would be a good time to call Shirley. I got up from my seat and headed into the kitchen where the telephone hung on the wall. I cranked the winder and got the operator.

"What number please?"

I gave her the number, and she connected me with my lovely ex.

"Hello."

"Hello, Shirley. This is Charlie."

"I know who you are, Charlie. You don't live with a person for ten years and not know his voice."

"You might not have recognized me on the telephone."

"I would know you if you yelled from the moon. Why did you call me?"

I figured I had better get on her good side first.

"Where are the kids?"

"They went with the neighbors camping. They'll be gone a couple of weeks."

"Oh, okay. I have some money for you. I'm sure you could use some money."

"Sure, what's the catch? I know you well enough to know that you need something when you do extra things for me."

"That's not true. I always gave you birthday cards and a valentine card every year that I could."

"I know, Charlie; you were sweet that way. But I still know you want something."

"All right, I'll come clean. Did you hear about the murder at the restaurant where I eat?"

"Yes, I know the place, and I did hear about it on the radio. Why?"

"Well it turned out that it wasn't just a robbery. The killer wanted to kill the lady that owned the place but killed her helper instead."

"What does that have to do with you and me?"

"I'm getting to that. I need to hide the lady that survived, and I would like for you to take her in for a few days."

"Why should I hide your girlfriend for you, Charlie?"

"I didn't say she was a girlfriend. She's just a person that needs protecting, that's all. I promise she'll be gone before the kids get home, okay?"

"You know I'm seeing someone?"

"I know; she won't get in your way. She'll be as quiet as a church mouse."

"I'll think about."

"Don't think about it too long. I need an answer really quick."

"All right, bring her over. I'll let her sleep in Lizzie's room."

"Thanks, Shirley. You're a class act. I know it was all my fault we couldn't get along."

I had to say that to keep her off guard.

"Yes it was, Charlie. You know how the war changed you."

"It changed all of us, Shirley, only some got worse. I'm sorry about that. I'll give you a call when I'm coming over."

"Okay, I'll talk to you later."

I hung up the telephone just as the girls were coming through the door.

"Who are you talking to, Charlie?" Mom asked.

"Just someone downtown. I need to talk to Maggie a minute."

"I'm sure that will be all right with her. May I ask what it's about?"

"I need to find another place for her to stay. I figure if I keep moving her around, it will be harder for someone to find her."

"That sounds logical. When will she leave?"

"That's what I want to talk to her about."

"I'll leave you two alone for a while then."

Mom went into the living room.

I took Maggie by the hand and led her to the table where I sat her down.

"I found a new place for you to stay. The only thing is it's at my ex-wife's house. She said you could stay."

"I guess it wouldn't be any worse than listening to your mother talk about her. I could see her in person."

"It won't be long. I'm going to find out who killed Hazel. You can count on that."

"I believe you, Charlie, but here the police are still outside guarding the house."

"I know, but they won't be able to stay too much longer."

"If you think it's best, then I'll do it."

"Okay, great. You go get your things together, and I'll call Shirley and let her know we're coming."

Maggie went to the bedroom to gather her things. I called Shirley to let her know we would be there in a couple hours.

I walked outside and across the street where John's man was standing. I let him know that I was moving Maggie and I would let John know where I took her.

I put Maggie in my car, and we drove off. She was especially quiet. That makes for a long trip when you're riding with someone that doesn't talk much. Usually, she was a blabbermouth, but I guessed she was really scared.

I asked Maggie if she minded if we made a stop at the airport. I explained why I needed to stop, and she said she didn't mind. We made our stop at the airport, and I told Maggie she should come in with me. She would be safer coming in with me than staying in the car. I still had to be careful that no one followed us.

We parked in the lot at the airport and walked into the terminal lobby. The building was very large, built with blocks that were cut from stone. It had large glass windows in the roof to cut down on lighting costs.

However, there were also lights hanging from the ceiling for night lighting. I liked the idea of free lighting mostly. That seemed pretty smart to me. With the cost of electricity going up all the time, you don't have to worry about the sun charging you. Why, my electric bill was three dollars and seventy-three cents last month. But what can you do.

I turned to Maggie.

"I have to find out what flight Captain Wodervull took to Alamogordo, New Mexico. I guess we should start with the clerk at the desk."

"Why do you need to know that?" she asked.

"I need to totally clear him as a suspect in this case."

"Do you think he could be guilty of something?"

"At this point, I'm not ruling out anyone."

"I guess it's possible that anyone could have done it."

"Let's see if we can get some info out of this clerk. Sometimes they don't like giving out information to anyone but the police. That's when my private cop license comes in handy."

We made our way to the counter. There was a nice-looking girl attending the post. She had big brown eyes and wore her hair in a bun close to the back of her head. She looked really good even in the standard work clothes they gave all their employees.

"Hi," I said. I looked at her name tag. "Karen, is it?"

"Yes, sir. Can I help you with something?"

"I hope so. I need to know if a Captain Wodervull took a flight from here to Alamogordo, New Mexico, on December 15."

"Are you sure he flew with Continental?"

"I'm not sure who he flew with. I just started here because you were the closest to me when we came in. Can you check some files to see if he was on that flight?"

"Why do you want to know? I'm not allowed to look into a file for just anyone."

"I'm a private cop looking into a murder that took place that day."

I took out my credentials for her to see. She looked curiously at them for a minute.

"I'll give it a look. I guess it will be okay."

She went to another room and was gone about five minutes. She emerged with a solemn look on her face. "I'm sorry, sir. We have no record of anyone by that name flying with us on that day. You might try Safeway Airlines. They offer the same ride for about three dollars less. I don't know how they can call themselves safer when everyone knows Continental is the safest airlines in the country."

"I don't either," I said to her. "Come on, Maggie. Let's try Safeway and see what we can find out."

We walked down the corridor to Safeway's counter. There was another bubbly girl on duty similar to the one I just talked to. I guess all airlines order them the same.

We walked up to the counter, and I said hi and gave her the same spiel that I gave the other lady. She went to another room and searched her files. When she came back, she was smiling. That was a good sign.

"We did have a Captain Wodervull fly with us that day."

"Do you remember what he looked like?"

"He was about five foot ten, tall, and had dark blue eyes."

"How do you remember that?"

137

"Because he had a military identification and wanted to fly standby. I told him there wouldn't be any problem. We had plenty seats available that day. Besides, I have never seen eyes like his. They were real dark for blue eyes."

"Thank you," I said. "You have been a big help."

I took Maggie by the arm, and we walked down the hallway.

"Did you get the information you wanted?" Maggie said.

"I sure did. That was our Captain Wodervull. The dark blue eyes did it for me. I'm positive that info clears him."

We took that information and headed to Shirley's house.

Maggie was beginning to look worried from all of this. She needed her life to get back to normal. I knew she missed working, and being away from her restaurant was driving her crazy. I could understand that. I just about lost my mind sitting and waiting on customers when I started my private-eye business.

Like my mother always said, "Idle hands makes for the devil's workshop." I suppose that means if you're not busy working you could get into a lot of trouble. I can see where that could work like that.

We got to Shirley's, and she was busy getting ready for her guest. Maggie wasn't too keen on the idea, but she felt she had no choice. I thought she would be safe there.

Maggie knew Shirley was my ex-wife, so we decided to play it cool and not let Shirley know we were seeing each other. It really would be better that way.

I got Maggie all settled in and headed out in search of new clues.

CHAPTER 21

I had to find someone that knew the two cousins. I know Captain Wodervull said he got along really well with his cousin James, but it wouldn't hurt to have someone confirm that.

I don't think Leslie will tell me much. I still think she's hiding something herself. The only other thing I can think of is to talk to someone back east that knew them growing up.

I headed back to my office to make a few phone calls. I needed to take care of Jerry before I did anything.

I arrived at my office. The place was still the same; nothing had been bothered. I picked up my telephone. It still worked. I placed a call to the hospital. A beautiful voice came on the other end of the line.

"County General Hospital, may I help you?"

"Can you ring Jerry Williams's room?"

"I'll ring the nurses' station on his floor. Can you hold a second?"

"Yes."

"Nurses' station."

"Can I speak to Jerry Williams?"

"What is your name?"

"Just tell him Charlie is calling."

I waited on the line what seemed to be five minutes.

"Hello," Jerry said.

"Jerry, this is Charlie."

"I know. They told me it was you. What's going on?"

"I called to see if you'll be discharged soon."

"The doctor said I could go home today."

"That's great. I'll be over to pick you up in about an hour."

"Okay, I'll be ready when you get here."

I hung up the phone and walked to where the coffee pot was sitting on the stove. I took the lid off and looked in. The coffee looked as if it could walk to me. I opted to leave it where it was. I'd grab a cup of coffee on the way to the hospital.

The drive took me about thirty minutes. The hospital parking lot was full as usual. *I think this must be one of the favorite places to go—or so it seems*, I thought. I noticed a car pulling out of a space. I made a mad run for it before some car came out of the ground to grab it. That's how fast you can lose a parking space if you snooze.

I got the old Ford parked and walked to the hospital lobby. The same lady was at the reception desk.

"I've seen you before," she said. "Who is it you want to see?"

Before I could answer, the elevator door opened, and Jerry walked out.

"Never mind, madam. He's here now."

"Oh, maybe I can help you next time," she said with a bright smile.

I smiled back. Jerry walked up to where I was standing.

"Ready to go home?" I said.

"You bet I am. I couldn't take another day of hospital food. I think they try to starve you to death."

"I know what you mean. How would you feel about staying at Blackie's home for a few days?"

"I don't know. Do I need to?"

"I think it would be best. The cops are still looking for the guy that took a shot at you and ran you off the road."

"Do they have any leads yet?"

"No, they don't have much to go on as of yet. How about you? Do you remember anything new about that night?"

"That night is still foggy in my mind. The doctor said things would slowly come back to me."

"So what do you think about staying with Blackie? He said you could have the place to yourself. He's at the bar most of the time, he told me."

"I guess it will be okay. I do need some time to get my strength back. You know how a bullet can take it out of you."

"That I do, Jerry."

I drove Jerry to Blackie's bar. We went inside to talk to Blackie for a minute.

Blackie was busy serving his early alcoholics. We chatted with Blackie for a few minutes. Blackie gave Jerry his key, and we left the bar. Blackie lived above the bar. That was a good deal; that way he would be close if anything happened.

I helped Jerry up the steps to the apartment. We went inside. Jerry sat down at the kitchen table.

"You should be okay here until I unravel this thing. Oh, I wanted to ask you what you know about James Mudd and his cousin Captain Wodervull? Do you know if they got along with each other?"

"I didn't know them too well, but I got the idea that there was a little competition between them."

"Why is that?"

"I couldn't pinpoint anything specific. It was just a feeling I got."

"Do you think either one could be capable of murder?"

"Anything is possible when a person is feeling trapped. Do you have a clue that points toward Captain Wodervull?"

"No, Gus had mentioned that Wodervull could have faked a flight out that day and killed his cousin. It would be difficult because he has a pretty good alibi for that time."

"I guess that clears Wodervull. I guess Gus thought he was being helpful when he mentioned that."

"You're probably right," I said. "It's just that I have nothing more to go on, and I don't want to wait until he kills someone else."

"I hope something turns up soon too. I wouldn't want to have to live with Blackie for the rest of my life." Jerry chuckled.

"Try not to worry about that now. Just concentrate on getting better."

"I feel good. Things are still coming back to me that I had forgotten. The doctor said I should have a full recovery."

"That's good. I need to get going, so I'll check on you in a couple days."

I left Jerry in Blackie's hands. I knew he would be taken care of there. I drove to my office to check on my mail.

I had an electric bill and a few advertisements. Nothing special.

I picked up the telephone and asked the operator to connect me with Alamogordo, New Mexico. She connected me with Captain Wodervull at the army post.

The captain answered the phone.

"Captain Wodervull."

"Hello, Captain. This is Charlie McQuillen."

"How are you doing, Charlie? What can I help you with?"

"I just wanted to let know that they cleared you in the murder of your cousin. I was pretty sure you weren't guilty, but I still needed to clear you."

"I'm glad to hear that. Do you have any clues yet as to who might have committed the crime?"

"I don't have any more than I had when I talked to you the other day. I did talk to Gus about the murder though."

"Gus? What did he have to say?"

"Not much. I thought for a minute he was trying to implicate you."

"Why would he do that?"

"I'm not sure. I guess he was looking for answers too."

"I suppose so. Well keep me updated on what's going on."

"I will. I'll call you. Bye."

I hung the phone up and sat and thought about everything for a while.

I couldn't help but think about what Gus had asked. Why would he implicate the captain? *Maybe Gus knows something that I don't. If he does, why didn't he let me know what it was? All I have to go on at this point is a Hudson sedan, a driver no one can recognize, and one military officer pointing the finger at another officer, who appears to be innocent.*

I decided I needed to have another talk with Gus to see what else I could extract from him.

I had no luck getting Gus on the telephone. *It seems he's away from his desk a lot these days*, I thought. *I can't help wonder what part Gus might be playing in this. Could it be possible that Gus is involved? I have no real reason to think so.*

I got back on the phone to Captain Wodervull. I had to ask him a few more questions.

The operator rang me through to the captain. He picked up the phone.

"Captain, this is Charlie McQuillen again. I wanted to ask you a couple more questions."

"Okay, go ahead."

"How well did your cousin James know Gus Harden?"

"I don't know how well he knew Gus, but I do know that he did know him. Maybe you should ask James's ex-girlfriend. She would know better than I."

"Do you know if they had any business dealings together?"

"I think they might have had something they were doing together."

"Do you know what it was?"

"I sure don't. I did want to tell you that I have been transferred back to my old job at the post. I'm leaving here tonight and will be at the post tomorrow."

"That's good. It will be easier to keep you informed on what's going on."

I was still on the phone when my buddy big Huey Johnson walked through the door. He walked to my desk and had a seat. I thought the chair might fold up under him.

"Doing any business these days?" Huey said.

"Some. Let me finish my call."

He nodded okay.

I said my good-byes to the captain.

"What's on your mind, Mr. Johnson?

"Mr. Wortts sent me to tell you he wants to see you and he won't take no for an answer."

"Do know what it's about?"

"Not a clue. He just told me to find you and convince you to come see him."

"Being you put it that way, I guess I can't say no. Where should I meet him?"

"I'll pick you up later and take you to him. He wants to keep this meeting private."

"Sounds serious."

"Mr. Wortts is always serious. He wants to wait until after dark to meet. How about I meet you here in the parking lot at eight thirty tonight?"

"You're the boss. See him then."

CHAPTER 22

I sat and waited until eight fifteen. I got up from my old ragged desk and headed down the steps to the outside. I stood by the door, and sure enough, big Huey pulled in the parking lot at eight thirty. He pulled up to the door where I was standing. He rolled down the window on the right side of the car. I guess he wanted to impress me that his car had electric windows. He kept the outside of his car spotless. It was hard to find dirt anywhere. I wondered if the inside was as clean as the outside.

"Get in," Huey said.

I opened the door and climbed in. I wondered no more. The car was spotless inside.

We drove for about twenty minutes, and Huey never said a word.

"Where are we going?"

"You'll know when we get there."

We finally turned onto a street that I recognized. It was Aloma. We drove to an alley and turned into it. It was the same building the two goons took the redhead to the night I followed them.

"Whose place is this?"

"It all belongs to Mr. Wortts. They make clothes here that they ship all over the world. Mr. Wortts is a very rich man and usually gets what he wants."

"I can understand that," I said.

He drove to the back of the building and parked.

"Lock that door. I don't want any bums lying in my car when we come out."

I pushed the lock down on the door and shut it.

"Mr. Wortts is waiting for you inside. Follow me."

I followed Huey inside the building. We walked down a long hallway to the back of the building. There were some small offices set aside. I could see a couple men sitting inside one of them. Huey led me to the office and opened the door. I could tell at that moment that one of the men was Mr. Wortts.

"Come in, Mr. McQuillen. Have a seat."

I walked in and found a seat. You could tell the chair had been used a lot. It looked old, worn, and dirty. Mr. Wortts sat in a chair behind the desk. The desk had plenty years on it too. It looked nothing like the plush desk that sat in his law office. This was a factory, and there was no need to keep up appearances.

"I know you're wondering why I brought you here in such a secretive way."

"The thought did cross my mind."

"I won't waste your time. I'll get right to what I want."

I nodded my head in agreement.

"The story I told you about the blackmail. Well, there's more to it than what I said. You know my daughter, Leslie. After she found out she didn't need to blackmail me, she dropped that.

"I have another problem I need help with. Someone is blackmailing me on another matter. If that gets out, it could create big problems for me in my run for the Senate. I need you to find out who this guy is."

"What happens then?"

"I convince him to go away."

"Like you did when you sent two of your goons to work me over?"

"That wasn't my doing. That was my daughter, Leslie. Those guys were only there to protect her. I guess they thought you got a little too close."

"What about the other guy following her?"

"I know nothing about that."

"I saw her and her bodyguards leaving her apartment one night with a folder that looked like it contained some paperwork. Do you know if that was part of her blackmail?"

"The folder contained her birth certificate naming me as her father and some letters from me to her mother when she was very young. Like I told you, we cleared that up, and it should no longer be a problem."

"How did you convince her to drop it?"

"I got her a good job, and I gave her $2,500 a month."

"That would do it. You don't consider that as blackmail?"

"No, she's my daughter, and it's the least I can do. After all, I wasn't around when she was small. Can you help me? How does $500 a week sound? Plus expenses?"

"That sounds pretty good. You do know that I'm working on a case involving the murder of Captain Mudd?"

"Yes, Leslie informed me. He was a nice person, but there's no conflict of interest there. The two cases shouldn't be connected."

"Okay, I suppose you're right. If you can't tell what you're being blackmailed about, what can you tell me?"

"I can tell you that I'm instructed to put $5,000 in a place that he chooses each month. He changes the location each time."

"He doesn't want you to get used to going to the same spot each time. That makes it harder to catch him."

"That's what I figured."

"I guess that's pretty smart. One thing about it, he will slip up somewhere. You can't blackmail someone forever."

"I thought about offering him a lump-sum payoff, but that wouldn't stop him from coming back later and asking for more. That's why I need you to find out who he is and give his name to me."

"Why don't you turn it over to the cops?"

"I don't want the police involved for the same reason I can't tell you what it's all about."

"I see. Did you ever see a vehicle after you dropped off the cash?"

"No, he was very careful. I never saw him or his vehicle. He told me if I nose around too much, it could get rough for me. So I'm a little afraid to try, but someone like you may be able to."

"Okay, suppose I take the job. I want you to understand if there turns out to be a conflict of interest, I would have to drop you as a client."

"I do understand that, but like I said, there shouldn't be a problem."

"Tell me something. You say you don't have any idea who it was following your daughter, yet he stopped following her after she came to see me. Maybe that person had something to do with Captain Mudd's murder."

"You could be right. I don't know anything that would help you there either."

"Are you sure it wasn't one of your boys you sent to guard her?"

"I'm positive it wasn't one of them. It was after she came to you that I sent my boys, as you say, to watch over her. I wanted her to be safe."

"Of course," I said. "I'll look into it for you."

"That sounds good."

He reached into his pocket and pulled out some bills.

"Will five hundred be enough retainer?"

All of a sudden, I felt rich. After all, Captain Wodervull gave me two hundred, and now Wortts handed me five big ones. Not to mention the five hundred Huey gave me. I still didn't know what that was about. Sometimes it's better not to ask any questions.

"Let me ask you something. How do I contact you if I find out anything?"

"Just call my office and say you have information about the Wilson case, and I'll meet you here about this same time on that same night."

"All right, that will work."

He got up from his seat and turned to Huey.

"Take Mr. McQuillen back to his car."

He then turned to me.

"I'll be expecting to hear from you," Wortts said.

"I'll do my best. It may take some time, you know. Let me know when you are supposed to meet this guy again."

"I will. Good-bye, Mr. McQuillen."

I waved good-bye. Huey escorted me out of the room.

We made our way back to Huey's fine Chrysler convertible.

At the moment, I had no glue as to how I was going to proceed on the thing. I just knew that a lot of people had given me a lot of money to figure it out, and I didn't seem to be any closer than I was when it first started. *I'm due a break here,* I thought. *Maybe one will come soon.*

We climbed into Huey's car, and he drove me back to my office where my old Ford sat in the parking lot. I got out of the car and said, "See ya," to Huey. As I walked to my car, it made me think that I needed a new vehicle to drive. *I've grown used to this one and I would hate to get rid of her,* I thought. *I could have her rebuilt and keep her. That's what I'll do.*

With that settled, I went up to my office to call and check on Maggie and Shirley. I didn't want them to think I had deserted them.

I walked into my office. I flipped the light switch on. The air was muggy warm from the day's heat. I went over and raised the window. That's when I noticed the black Hudson parked on the street. He had parked where the light was dim. There was no way of seeing who the person was that was driving it. There seemed to be someone sitting in the passenger's seat. I knew the man standing had noticed me looking at him.

I grabbed the heater from my inside jacket pocket and ran for the steps. This would be a great time for the elevator to work, but the damn thing was still out of service. Down five flights of stairs I went. I ran out into the street. The man jumped into the Hudson and tore out. There was no way I could get to my car and catch up to him. I knew I still had a problem, not to mention Jerry and Maggie. I told myself I had to let them know that the guy was still on the loose and they could still be in serious danger. I knew they'd be upset by that news.

I slowly made my way back up the steps to my office. Those stairs seemed to be getting harder to climb.

I figured I had better stay away from the window this time just in case the guy made a return engagement to kill me. I turned the light back out. I could talk on the phone in the dark. That would be much safer. The operator rang Shirley's number for me.

"Hello," she said.

"Shirley, this is Charlie."

"Do tell, what do you want this time of night, Charlie?"

"I need to talk to Maggie. Is she still up?"

"Yes, I'll get her."

I waited what seemed like an hour even though I knew it was only a couple of seconds.

"Hi, Charlie. What's going on?"

"Don't get scared, but the guy that ran me off the road?"

"Yes, what about him?"

"I just saw the same car parked on the street below my office. He was sitting there watching for me. So I think it's best you stay there with Shirley for a few more days."

"Okay, Charlie, but isn't there a way I could go back to work at the restaurant? I'm getting awful nervous not being able to go to work."

"I know you are, and I'll try to fix a way for you to go to work as long as you leave before it gets dark and watch out for anyone that is driving a black Hudson."

"A black Hudson. Why a black Hudson?"

"That's the kind of car that ran me off the road and the same kind of car that my mysterious man was driving tonight."

"I know someone that had a car like that."

"You do. Who?"

"It was that captain that used to date Leslie Carworth. The lady that worked for Peter's brother."

"Do you mean Captain Mudd?"

"I think that was his name."

"Are you sure? It must have belonged to one of his friends. He's dead, and the car is still running around."

"I know. You must be right. So who would it belong to?"

"I don't know. My friend at the army post might know. He knew Captain Mudd. He may be able to give some idea."

"Charlie, just be careful. I don't want you to get killed on my account."

"I'll be very careful. Besides, it's not your fault that this is happening. It started way before you got involved. You girls just stay out of sight for a few days. I got a new lead I'm working on. Okay?"

"Okay, we will. That is, if Shirley doesn't get tired of me."

I heard Shirley in the background saying, "It's okay, Charlie. She can stay as long as she wants to."

"Okay," I said. "Tell Shirley I appreciate her doing this, and I'll be around to give her some more money for the kids as soon as I can."

"Shirley says that will be fine. She knows you and I are going together, so you don't have to walk on eggs around her anymore."

"Well that's a great load off my mind. I'll give you a call tomorrow. I don't think it would be wise to come out there just yet. I may be followed, and I don't want to lead him to you. Let me say something to Shirley."

"Okay," Maggie said.

"Hello, Charlie. How are you doing?"

"Fine. I want to ask you how the kids are doing."

"They're doing well. They're still at camp."

"Tell them I love them and I'll bring them a present when I see them again."

"I will. Bye, Charlie."

"Bye, Shirley."

I hung up the telephone and sat there for a while.

CHAPTER 23

I didn't want to fall asleep in my office, so I made myself get up and go to my quaint little apartment for a nap. Maggie telling me about seeing Captain Mudd in a Hudson threw me for a loop. I did know it wasn't him that ran me off the road that night. I'd have to find Captain Wodervull and ask him if he might know any of the friends that his cousin had that drove a Hudson. *This may be the glue I've been looking for—and to think that Maggie's had it in her pretty little head all the time*, I thought. *I just needed to say the right thing to bring it out.*

I fell asleep on my old army cot. It wasn't too bad, but someday I did intend on getting a good bed. At the age of forty-two, these things start to matter to you.

I was awakened by the sound of someone beating on my back door. I forced myself to get out of bed. I stopped by the kitchen sink on the way and turned the water on so I could splash some water on my face. You would be surprised what a little water on your face in the morning does for you. It tends to get me going as much as a good cup of coffee.

After I finished splashing my face, I walked over to the door and opened it.

"Oh, hi, Mrs. Kates. How are you this bright morning?"

"Just fine, just fine. I brought your laundry to you. I finally fished it last night."

"Great. I was sure in need of a clean shirt today. Oh much do I owe you?"

"A couple bucks will do."

"Just a minute."

I walked to my bedroom. I always put my wallet in a drawer beside my bed. I got out a five spot and headed back to the kitchen.

"Here you go. All I got is I five spot."

"Oh my goodness. I don't have any change on me."

"Don't worry about it. Consider the rest a tip for good service."

"Well, that's very nice of you, Mr. McQuillen. If there's anything more, you just let me know."

"Thank you, and I will, and you can just call me Charlie. I like that better."

"Okay, I will. I'll see you later."

"Bye, Mrs. Kates."

I shut the door and took my laundry to the bedroom. A good shower and some clean clothes would be a good start to the day.

I had to go quiz some folks on some things, and I'd just as soon feel good while doing it.

It took me about thirty minutes to finish my business in the bathroom.

I called Maggie and told her not to worry. I told her I had some new clues I had to follow up on and this thing should be cleared up real soon. Of course, that was stretching it a little, but I didn't want her to worry.

I got myself ready and headed for the army post. Maybe I would be lucky enough to catch Gus. Gus was a busy guy with the job he did, so it would be just good luck if I caught him.

I drove up the gate about a half hour later.

"Who do you need to see today, Charlie?"

"Colonel Gus Hardin."

He wrote my name down in his book along with the name of the person I was there to see.

"Okay, you know where to go."

"Thanks, Mike. I won't be long. I'll see you on the way out."

He waved me through. I drove straight to where Gus's office was. I parked and walked into the building. The sergeant was busy as usual banging away on his typewriter. After he finished typing, he looked up.

"Oh, it's you. If you're here to see Gus today, you're in luck. He's in his office. I'll see if he can see you."

"I do need to see Gus."

I picked up a magazine that was lying on the desk.

He got up from his desk and went into Gus's office. He was back in a few seconds.

"Gus says to come on in his office."

I laid the magazine down and walked into Gus's office.

Gus was sitting at his desk. I noticed the insignia on his collar. He had been promoted to full-bird colonel.

"When did this happen?" I said, pointing to his collar.

"I got the orders yesterday."

"That's great, Gus. You deserve it. You've been a great soldier for many years."

"Thank you, Charlie. Maybe in a few more years I'll make general. For now, I'll be happy with this rank."

"Hey, being a colonel is not doing too bad."

"Yeah, you're right. What did you want to see me about?

"I wanted to ask you about Captain Mudd. Do you know if he drove a dark-colored Hudson at one time or another?"

157

"I don't know if he had a car or not. It seems to me that he mostly rode in a cab. I think there were a couple of times that his cousin came by and picked him up. I believe he drove a dark-colored vehicle."

"I never knew about the cousin until I got to investigating Captain Mudd's murder," I said.

"I only knew of him through Captain Mudd. Did you know that James told me that his cousin used to be a pretty good actor before he joined the service?"

"Is that so? Maybe he's been putting on and act for me too."

"What do you mean?"

"He asked me to look into the murder of Captain Mudd for him. He even gave me a couple hundred bucks to get started. So if he owns a Hudson, then he has some explaining to do."

"How's that?"

"Well, it was a guy in a black Hudson that ran me off the road, and the same car was seen leaving the scene of another crime. Not to mention the guy that tried to kill Jerry. I think it was all the same person."

"How's Jerry doing?"

"He's fine. I have him at Blackie's. Blackie said he could stay there until this was solved. I didn't want Jerry to stay at his own home—just in case the guy tried to kill him again."

"That's smart. You never can be too careful. I heard there was a killing at Maggie's place. What happened there?"

"Someone tried to rob the place. They wound up killing Hazel, Maggie's waitress. It turned out the vehicle was the same car that was involved in the other assaults."

"Gee, that's something. Where is Maggie now?"

"I got her staying with Shirley for now."

"Is that wise? You know how women are. They can't get along when they're friends for very long, let alone when one is a girlfriend and the other is an ex-wife. I got to admit, no one would think to look there for Maggie if they still wanted to knock her off."

"That was my thought too. I guess my next thing to do is to find Captain Wodervull and get a few answers from him and inform him that I no longer can work for him. At least until I find out if he indeed does drive a Hudson."

"Whatever you do, Charlie, you had better watch your back. If he is the killer, he may try to get you too."

"I think he already tried last night."

"Oh, why is that?"

"I saw a black Hudson outside my office building last night. I didn't let them get the jump on me, so they left in a hurry."

"What do you mean they?"

"There were two guys in the automobile."

"Did you get a look at either one of them?"

"Not really. They were too far away when I saw them. I was standing looking out my window, and they were on the street. By the time I got downstairs, they had already gone."

"Tough luck, Charlie. If you had recognized them, you could have turned them over to the police."

"Yeah, this thing is wearing me down. I know the girls have to be tired and scared. Well, Gus, I need to get going. We'll have to meet at Blackie's when this is over, and I'll buy you a drink."

"That sounds like a good idea. Be careful, Charlie. I'll let you know if I think of anything else."

"Okay, here's my office number."

Gus handed me his address book.

"Just write it down in here."

"I'll give you both numbers just in case you need to contact me afterhours. The number on the bottom is my home telephone. Oh, there was something else I wanted to ask you. Have you seen Captain Wodervull since he returned to duty here?"

"Uh, no. I haven't had a chance to talk to him. I really didn't know he was in town."

"He called me and told me he was returning to duty here and he would be in contact with me. Well anyway, if you see him, tell him to give me a call. Don't let on like I'm suspicious about anything."

"I'm not a good actor, but I'll try," Gus said.

"Great. Then I'll catch you later. I'm going to stop by the police station and check in with John. I need to fill him in on what I found out."

"See ya later, Charlie."

I left Gus's office and boarded my old Ford and headed for John's office. It was about a half-hour drive back to the police station where John spent most of his time.

It was a nice warm day, so I drove along with the window down. There is something good about driving with the windows down. Of course, when I smoked cigarettes, I had the window open winter and summer. *Boy, it feels good to be off them things,* I thought. I thought I would never be able to quit. You really have to put your mind to it to get it down.

I rolled up to the police station. I parked in an open spot and went inside. I made my way to John's office where he was sitting at his desk talking on the phone.

He was wearing a white shirt with blue stripes. I think it must be the only shirt he has, unless he has a lot of the same kind. He never wore a tie. His slacks were black dress pants. The pants you wear don't matter too much. You can get by wearing the same pants a couple days in a row.

He said good-bye to someone and hung up the phone.

"You're just the guy I need to see," John said.

"Oh, really. I had the same idea, I guess. I have some information I need to tell you about."

"I just got a call from Traffic. They found a black four-door sedan busted all up. It seems it ran off the road somewhere in Topanga Canyon. They want me to go check it out when they bring it up to see if there might have been foul play involved. It could be your black Hudson you've been looking for," John said.

"That's what I wanted to talk to you about. It seems that Captain Mudd was seen in a black Hudson on occasion. We both know that it can't be Captain Mudd that was later seen driving away from a couple crime scenes, so who was it?"

"I have no clue at the moment. Go with me, and we'll talk about it on the way."

We left the building, talking on the way.

"I may be able to identify the driver if it is indeed the same Hudson. I got an idea I already know who it is."

"How do you know that?" John asked.

"It's part of what I found out recently. Unless I missed my guess, I think it may be Captain Wodervull in the Hudson. He's Mudd's cousin. The same guy that hired me to find Mudd's murderer."

We entered John's cruiser and headed toward Topanga Canyon. It took us about forty minutes to reach the area where they had pulled the vehicle up to the road. We pulled over and parked. We got out and walked over to the battered car. It was a Hudson all right. But was it the same Hudson we're looking for?

John walked over to one of the officers that was standing there.

"Did someone notify the coroner?"

"Yes, they tell me he's on his way. I guess he wasn't too busy today. We got a quick response this time," the officer said.

We stood around about another twenty minutes, and the coroner's wagon came driving up.

He pulled up close to where the Hudson sat and parked. I supposed he didn't like to have to walk to far.

He retrieved his coroner's bag from his backseat and headed to the Hudson. It didn't take him long to pronounce the man dead.

He walked over to where John and I were standing.

"You can take him out of the auto now. He's very dead."

He has a very strange sense of humor, I thought. *I think coroners are strange anyway.*

We had to wait on a crew to come to pry the body out of the Hudson. It was pretty mangled.

"I guess you're here to check for foul play, John," the doctor said.

"Yeah, did you see any bullet hole in him anywhere?"

"No, but I didn't check too close. I knew you needed to look the body over too."

"That's always the worst part of my job."

The ambulance pulled up. Along with them came the crew to take the body out if necessary. It looked as if it would be necessary. John was trying to open the Hudson's door. He was having no luck.

After the crew removed the body from the wreck, the ambulance crew put him on a cart.

One of the medics motioned for John to come and see what he discovered.

"This guy has been shot."

"I guess that settles that. Come here, Charlie. Take a look and see if this is your guy."

I walked over to the cart and took a look.

"That's Wodervull all right. I thought I had this thing solved, and now I find my top suspect dead from a bullet wound."

"I'm sure the fall down the canyon didn't help him either," John said.

I stood there dumbfounded, not knowing where to turn next. *Jerry and the girls won't be happy about this. This means they'll have to stay in hiding a little longer.*

"Maybe we can get some fingerprints off the vehicle."

The ambulance crew and the wrecking crew both used caution dealing with the wrecked car, making sure to not to get any of their prints on the vehicle. They were used to dealing with police procedures. If there was foul play, the killer might have left a print somewhere on the automobile.

"Where do you go from here, Charlie?"

"I suppose back to my office to try to call Leslie Carworth and see what she knows about Captain Wodervull."

I didn't want to tell John about me working for Mr. Wortts just yet. At this point, I didn't know if Wortts's men might have done this job.

"Okay, get him out of here," John said.

The crew loaded him into the ambulance and headed to town. The wrecking crew continued to hook up the car for transport to a wrecking yard.

John and I got in his police cruiser and drove off toward the station. We drove along talking.

"Charlie, why don't you come over this weekend? Marge and I are having a cookout, and you're invited."

"Are you sure Marge won't mind?"

"I'm sure. She likes you and Shirley."

"She does remember that Shirley and I aren't together anymore, doesn't she?"

"She knows. I guess she's hoping that you two will get back together again."

"I don't think there's a chance for that. Besides, Shirley has a new boyfriend now."

"Anybody we know?"

"I don't know; she won't tell me who he is. She thinks I'll try to waylay the guy or something. You know how women are."

"I sure do. Marge and I have been together for twenty-five years now. I don't know what I would do without her."

"Yeah, you two have been together so long you're beginning to look alike."

"You're crazy, Charlie."

John pulled up to the police precinct. We parked and got out of the cruiser.

"I'll talk to you later, John. I'm going to my office and make a few phone calls." I got in my old Ford and drove off.

It didn't take me long until I was back at my office climbing the long stairway to the fifth floor. I reached the top. Mr. Mire, the building super, was standing there.

"Why didn't you use the elevator, Charlie? You know we got it fixed, don't you?"

"No, I didn't, but that's good to know. That's a long climb up these stairs."

"I'll say. It just about wore me down to nothing trying to keep up with all the chores in this building."

"Yeah, maybe you'll get to feeling better now. It was tough on me when I was injured in that wreck I had."

"Did you ever find out who ran you off the road?"

"I think I may have found out who he was today."

"That's good. Do they have him in jail?"

"Don't need to. He's dead."

I thought, *I won't have to drop him as a client now.* I still had Mr. Wortts though.

"Well, I need to take care of some business, Fred. I'll see you later.

I opened my office door and walked in. Nothing had changed. It was the same old crummy-looking office. *If jobs keep coming in like they have been, I'll find a more suitable place,* I thought. *For now, I'll have to see.*

CHAPTER 24

The office didn't smell too bad. I had left the window open the night before, and the stuffiness was all gone. I usually put it down because you never know when it may rain in Los Angeles. I know people that leave their convertible tops down most of the time. They're a trusting bunch.

I picked up the phone and had the operator dial Mr. Wortts's office number. His secretary answered.

"Wortts's law office. May I help you?"

"Yes, may I speak to Mr. Wortts?"

"May I say who is calling?"

"You may. This is Charlie McQuillen."

"I'll see if he can see you, Charlie. Just a minute."

I heard her drop the phone on the desk. She was gone for a few seconds, and then she retrieved the phone again.

"Hello, Charlie. Mr. Wortts will talk to you now. I'll put you through. Go ahead, Mr. McQuillen.

"Hello, Mr. Wortts. I would like to know if you heard from your blackmailer again."

"As a matter of fact, I did. He told me that he wanted me to give him $500,000 and he would never bother me again."

"I was afraid of that."

"Why?"

"I thought I had the blackmailer. The police found Captain Wodervull Hudson at the bottom of Topanga Canyon.

"Who?"

"Captain Wodervull. He was a cousin to Captain Mudd. Leslie's friend."

"Oh yes, I remember now."

"It was the same car that tried to run me off the road. I was hoping he was the blackmailer so I could tell you that I had this thing solved. What are your instructions this time?"

"He said he would call me later tonight with a place to make the payoff."

"Okay, I'll hang around the office today. As soon as you hear from him, let me know. This may be the only chance to catch him."

"Maybe I should just pay him off and hope he never bothers me again."

"I don't know about you, but I would want this thing stopped. You know that with paying him off he can come back anytime and want more money."

"I know that, but he sounded as if he really needed to get out of town in a big hurry."

"I'm sure he does. I think whoever he is, he was one of the men I saw outside my office. I also think he's probably the blackmailer. I think we need to catch this guy because he's killed a lot of people so far just to keep this quiet."

"I know, but this is just between you and me. I also need this guy dead. If he's caught alive, he'll tell what he has on me, and it will ruin the rest of my life."

"I won't agree to knock him off for you. There's nothing that could be worth that."

"I'm sorry you feel that way, Mr. McQuillen. I'll think over what you said, and if I think I can live with the outcome, I'll call you when I hear from him."

"Remember, you don't want to find yourself locked in a cell too. Do you?"

"I have to go, Mr. McQuillen."

He hung up the phone. I replaced my receiver on its hanger and leaned back in my chair. It was times like this that I wished I had never gotten into this business. I have to admit you meet a lot of good people and a lot of creepy people too.

I had been sitting in my chair for about ten minutes, thinking, when one of the people I was hoping to see showed up. It was the redhead Leslie Carworth.

"I have some questions to ask you, Mr. McQuillen."

"That's fair. I have some questions to ask you too. Like how much do you know about the blackmailing of your father?"

"What are you accusing me of? I know nothing of any blackmail. Especially of my own father. I would never be involved in something like that."

"Your part in this looks pretty suspicious."

"I don't care what you think. I have nothing to do with it. Aren't you supposed to be finding James's killer?"

"As a matter of fact, I think I have a clue who was involved in that. I'll know more when I find your father's blackmailer. Do you know anyone that was friends with James that drove a black Hudson?"

"Why, no. I don't know a Hudson from any other car."

She started to squirm when I brought up that question.

While we were sparring about what each other knew or didn't know, the phone rang. I grabbed for the telephone.

"Don't go away. I need to ask you more questions."

I answered the phone. It was Shirley on the line. She sounded like she was coming apart at the seams.

"Hello, Charlie. You have to come quick. Maggie and I need you right away."

"Calm down. What's the big problem? Are you at home?"

"No, here's the address. It's a cabin in the woods at 2394 Forest Road. Charlie, come alone and don't tell anybody else about this."

"What's this all about, Shirley? Are you and Maggie being held against you will?"

"I can't say any more. Just come as fast as you can."

I heard the phone slam down in my ear. I knew then that something was wrong. I put the receiver down and turned to the redhead.

"I have to go, but I may need to talk to you again. So don't get too lost.

"Who was that on the phone?" she asked.

"It was my ex-wife. I have to go take care of something."

I noticed her looking at the address I had wrote down.

"Is this where she lives?"

Somehow I think she already knew the answer to that question.

"I can't talk anymore. I have to go. Close the door on your way out.

I left the building in a hurry. I needed to get to the address Shirley gave me. I knew where the road was. There were mostly old cabins along there where people stayed when they wanted to get away from things.

I drove along as fast as I could without winding up in a ditch. I couldn't help the girls if I got in an accident before I got there. One thing I was pretty sure about was that they were in big trouble and someone was using them to get to me. Chances were I'd be getting a few answers and wouldn't be able to use them. *I believe this person intends on killing me, and I don't think he'll want to leave any witnesses.*

I pressed the old Ford as hard as I could, and I was trying to see the numbers on the boxes as I went past.

Twenty-three hundred. I was getting close. *There it is.* Twenty-three ninety-four.

I started back the long drive that led to the cabin. I thought I would get close and then walk on in, hoping to get a look at the situation before I stuck my foot all the way in. I needed to formulate a plan of action. I pulled to the side of the drive and parked. I shut the engine off. Hopefully no one heard me. I couldn't see the cabin yet, so maybe I was safe. I got out of the old Ford and made my way to the cabin. I could see it come into view. I circled around and noticed a big black Buick sitting there. It looked like the same car that I saw pick up the redhead that night. I was now sure the she had something to do with this. I took my heater out of my pocket and made my way to a window. I looked in through the dirty glass. It looked as though no one had been here in a long time. I supposed that was why they had chosen the place.

I wasn't there very long before I felt this cold piece of iron against the back of my head. I turned around. It was the goon that tried to rough me up. The one I busted in the crotch.

"Don't try any funny stuff. I would love to do you right here, but the boss wants me to bring you inside."

"You got me, pal. Let's go see the boss."

I walked in front of the goon into the cabin. A shock was waiting there. I saw Shirley and Maggie there, both tied and gagged. But the biggest shock hadn't settled in yet.

"Gus, what the hell are you doing here?" I asked.

"Sorry, Charlie. I couldn't tell you my plans. I knew you wouldn't go along with them."

"How did you get involved in this?"

"Well, I tell you, Charlie, it goes way back to the war days. You see, I was stationed in Germany with Wortts, and after the war, he was put in charge of getting rid of German prisoners. He was told from higher-ups to—how should I say this—he was to dispose of all the prisoners in his charge. So he ordered me and a small company of men to slowly take this prisoner out and execute him. I was lucky enough to get the whole conversation on wire without him knowing about it. Oh, I took a few pictures too. Then after the war, I found out he was running for California Senator. I got myself transferred here. I figured as rich as this guy was, I might as well make a few bucks out of the deal too."

"What about James Mudd? Did you knock him off too?"

"Yeah, I really hated to do that. He was a nice guy, but he got too nervous about blackmailing old man Wortts. He wanted me to call it off, and I just couldn't do that. Say, you're asking a lot of questions."

"I figured that you're not going to let me get out of here, so I might as well get the whole picture from you."

"You see, my big pal here is going to town to create an alibi for me while I'm taking care of you. I put a mustache on him, and he'll pass for me anywhere."

"I agree that you two look alike under these circumstances."

I thought, *That's good. I'll only have Gus to contend with. There is no way I'm going to let him kill Shirley and Maggie. I'll wait until the big guy leaves before I try anything.*

Gus took a rope from a drawer and threw it to Harry. Harry is a tall skinny guy with brownish hair and brown eyes. Those eyes of his look a little shifty to me. His clothes are dirty and look as if he slept in them. I don't think I would trust old Harry out of my sight. However, if I do get out of this I think I'll keep Harry on my radar.

"Tie old Charlie up, Harry. We don't want him running around loose, do we?"

"Uh, no, boss."

I thought, *This will make things a little more difficult.* I had a knife in my front pocket, but there was no way I could get to it with Gus watching me all the time. Maybe luck would be with me. It had to.

Old Harry finally left the cabin, heading to town. I thought somehow I had to work fast because it wouldn't take him long to do what he had to do.

The girls were tied up and kept in one of the bedrooms. *This is a nice little cabin,* I thought. *I think after I get out of this, I may find me something like it.*

"What about Captain Wodervull? Who did him?" I said.

"I'm sorry about that one too. I needed him to feed me information through James. After he realized I knocked off James, he came after me, and I had to kill him too. I tried to get Maggie that night. I couldn't have her remembering me at old man Wortts that night. She was the only person that had gotten a good look at me."

"You should have left her alone. She would have never put it together. I don't think she knew who you were and wouldn't think you would've been involved in this," I said.

"I did make some mistakes, but I have them all figured out now. The only other guy I have to take care of is Jerry. I hate that. I liked him."

"Well I guess that just about clears everything up except what the redhead has to do with this."

Just then, we heard an automobile come roaring up. They left the engine running and ran through the door.

I guess we're just about to find out what the redhead has to do with it. She stared at the situation for a few seconds. She then turned to Gus in disgust.

"What the hell do you think you're doing? You never told me you were going to kill these people. You can't do that."

"That's not all, Ms. Carworth. He was fixing to take a half million dollars of your daddy's money and run out on you."

"You dirty bastard. I knew I shouldn't have trusted you. You said no one would get hurt."

About that time, she pulled out a stub-nosed .38-caliber revolver. She pumped four rounds into Gus's worthless hide.

She stood there in a daze. I decided I had better start talking fast before she came to and wanted to finish the job on us.

She was shaking like a leaf. Maggie and Shirley were screaming from the other room like they had been shot.

Leslie dropped the revolver to the floor. She started to gather her senses about her.

"I'm so sorry, Mr. McQuillen. I never wanted that to happen. I never intended for anyone to get killed."

"You did the right thing, Ms. Carworth. Gus was getting ready to finish us off when you came in. Can you untie me?"

"Sure," she said.

The redhead untied me, and I went in the other room and untied Shirley and Maggie.

"Charlie, I need to tell you something," Shirley said.

"What might that be?"

"The guy I was seeing was Gus. I just now figured out why he looked me up. He was always asking me questions about you. He told me not to say anything about us seeing each other. He said it would just complicate our friendship right now. Now I know he was just keeping an eye on you."

I hugged her.

"Don't worry about it now. This whole thing is finally solved."

I gave Maggie a big hug and a kiss. I decided I wasn't going to keep my relationship with Maggie from Shirley any longer.

Now all I had to worry about was catching old Harry in town. *I think I'll leave that up to the police to do that job.*

I searched around in Gus's stuff lying there. I found some files that looked like the evidence that he had on Mr. Wortts. I had to make a decision on whom to give it to. Mr. Wortts or the police. After all, Wortts was ordered to do what he did by higher-ups. Maybe it wasn't up to me to pass judgment on him.

EPILOGUE

I decided that Mr. Wortts should have all the information I found on Gus.

That decision turned out to be a good thing. Mr. Wortts offered me a deal I couldn't turn down. I'm on a $200 per week retainer. That will pay my bills. The great thing about it is I can still pursue other jobs that might come my way.

The last I heard from Detective John Garbor was they were still looking for old Harry. I'm sure he'll turn up somewhere in someone's pocketbook.

It's a new year, and things are looking good for a change.

CPSIA information can be obtained
at www.ICGtesting.com
Printed in the USA
LVOW12s2055291116

515012LV00002B/75/P